DEATHSBANE

LINDSEY RICHARDSON

AUTHOR'S NOTE

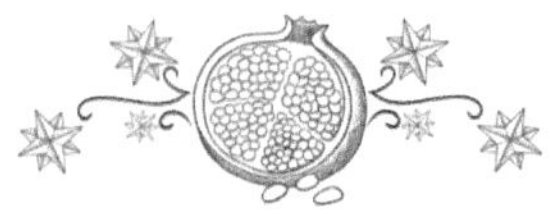

Deathsbane is a novella in the Godsbane universe. It is intended to be read second, and as such, contains major spoilers for Godsbane. <u>Please do not read *Deathsbane* if you have not read Godsbane.</u>

Deathsbane is a dark fantasy romance that contains adult themes, explicit language, violence, and sexual content that may not be appropriate for all readers. Reader discretion is advised. For a full list of these themes, please visit www.lindseyrichardsonau thor.com.

PRONUNCIATION GUIDE
GODS OF THE GOLDEN PANTHEON

- Drayven — *dray-ven*
- Selene — *suh-leen*
- Lyra — *leer-uh*
- Nina — *knee-nuh*
- Mikais — *mick-eye-is*
- Nobus — *no-bus*
- Arcasia — *ar-cay-zee-uh*
- Drayca — *dray-cah*
- Taura — *tar-uh*
- Bastin — *bass-tin*
- Seblee — *seh-blee*
- Gaius — *guy-us*
- Calaedon — *cal-aye-dun*

Major Gods of the Golden Pantheon

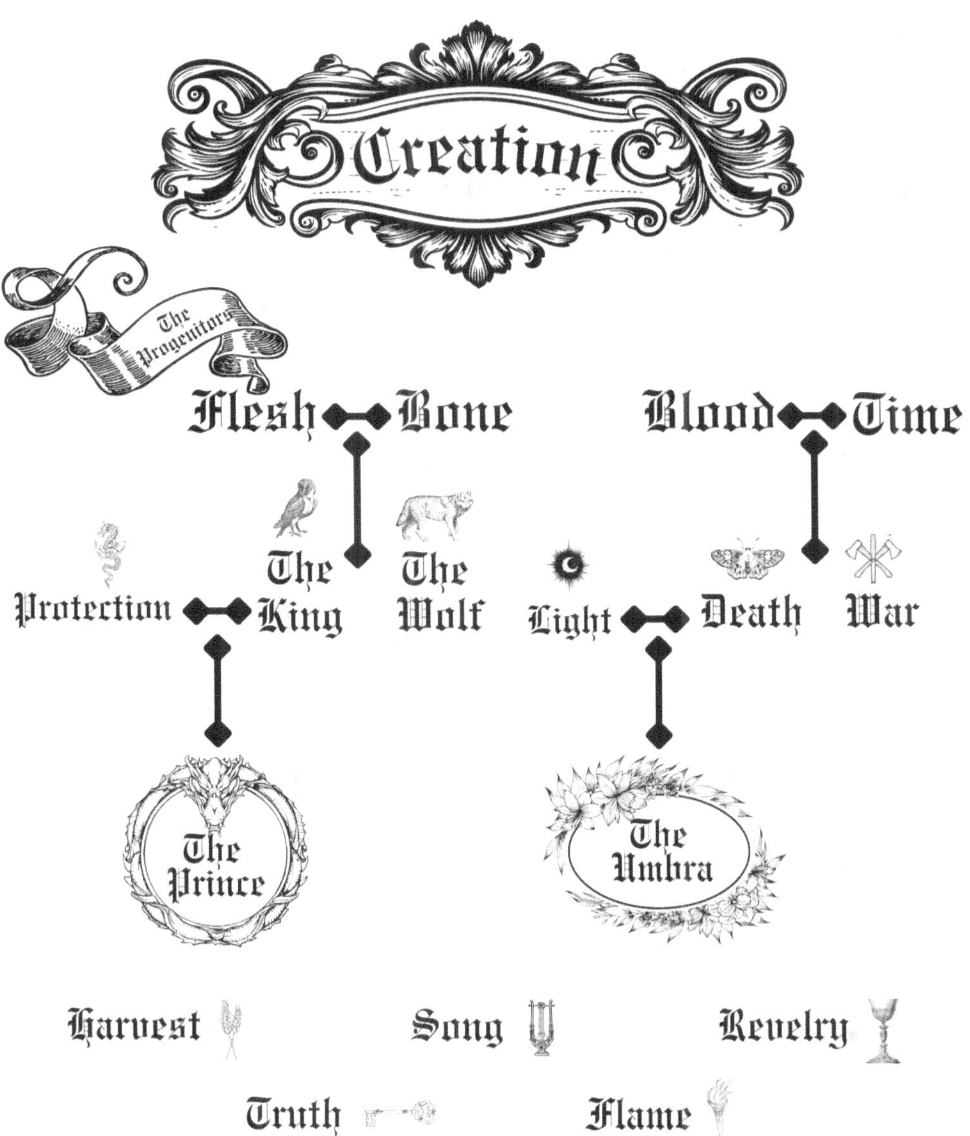

To be forgotten
is to be
powerless

CHAPTER 1

DEATH

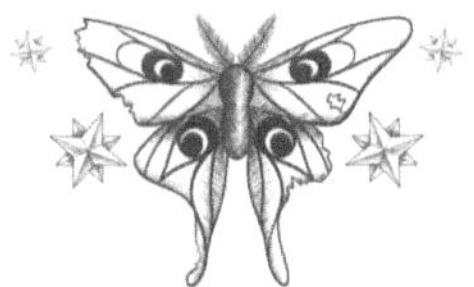

A funeral for a god has to be one of the most ridiculous fucking things I've seen in my eons of life. But then again, the simpering mortals around the funeral pyre don't know the cold body they're crying over is a god. To them, he is an apothecary—a mortal man with a pension for knowing the exact herbs and formulations to craft whatever tonic they believe will cure their ailments. They call him Gavin, none the wiser of his real name or powers.

Gaius the Green, God of Plants, is not known in this realm. A lesser deity, he's not particularly known in any realm, making his lack of worshippers a convenient excuse for his untimely demise. There is no more effective way to kill a god, after all, than to erase their existence from the minds of mortals. To be forgotten is to be powerless.

Few exist with the ability to kill a god any other way, and despite what others may think, I don't relish being amongst them. I may be the God of Death, but the other gods are just as dark. The ones who hunger most for power—Nobus, Mikais, and the ones who came before them—are the truly wicked ones. The Progenitors, the original four children of Creation, ensured we were all bred with ruthlessness and hunger in our veins. What else would you expect from Flesh, Bone, Blood, and Time?

To that, I am no exception. My mother, the Goddess of Blood herself, was the first god I killed. The acts that led me to matricide also led me to the bargain that ensured my eternal sentence: my life tied to that of my realm.

King of the Under Realm is a fancy, enviable title I claimed for myself. But I am a king only in name.

I am a warden, a jailer of souls held captive, forever unable to tell a living soul the terms of my servitude. The dark world of blood and bone comprises the bars of my eternal prison. Death may live in every realm, but only the Under Realm can sustain me —and no one but the dead can reside there.

Any day away from that prison costs me greatly, but today, I pay it willingly, if only to witness what unfurls before me now.

"Thank you for coming." The sweet voice floats on the late summer breeze, rising above the crowd of mourners. "We'll light the pyre at sunset."

Even in a realm that hides her shimmering skin, Selene shines. The Goddess of Light, with a head of luscious golden curls, cuts through the throngs of villagers like a beacon in the night. She bobs and weaves past them on a path that leads straight to me. The shadows that conceal me fall away as she approaches.

"Drayven."

Why am I not surprised that the only person in all of existence who still calls me by my birth name could sense me here, hidden and cloaked in night?

"When will you stop calling me that?"

"Considering it's been centuries since you asked me to, I would bet on never if I were you." White teeth flash in a hint of a smile that disappears as quickly as it arrived.

So few smile in the face of Death, and it's that unique trait that keeps me sucked into the goddess' orbit after all these years. No one is permitted to call me by that name, but there's a part of me, an infinitesimal part, that would be sad to never hear it again.

"Thank you for coming," she offers. "He always respected you. He understood that his power could not exist without your balance."

Her golden eyes find mine, tears rimming them. What is it like to have enough humanity to cry? The last tear I shed was a century ago.

"He was a good god." Always an ally, Gaius often felt like the only being who saw my curse as a gift—well, him and his eldest daughter. They're both fools.

"I grew as many plants on the pyre as I could. Familial magic isn't as strong in this realm. Perhaps that's why he chose this one for his home."

Magic in general isn't as strong here, but I don't correct her. Regardless of the realm, we're all outrunning the hereditary powers of our parentage, always desperate for a fleeting moment when we don't feel the crushing weight of our inheritance.

Gods are not made, they are born. Creation, the supremely divine source of life, chooses when a new god is needed, carefully selecting the specific traits of the parents to create exactly what is missing from the Golden Pantheon. Divinely crafted deities made only of the most optimal powers.

The gods of Blood and Time were not enough for Creation, and so the all-parent created me from their union. Death itself. I must admit—the ability to manipulate both is useful in executing my duty, but luckily for me, there is no need to create anything from death. The curse of my powers will never be passed to another, and for that, I am grateful.

The Goddess of Light holds up her hand and breathes deeply. Faint threads of green magic shimmer in the late afternoon sunlight as she channels what little plant magic she can summon. A dark purple bloom forms in her upturned palm, five midnight-hued sepals surrounding a cluster of yellow nectaries in its center.

Selene smiles at her creation, passing it to me. "They call it godsbane here. Such a silly name for a flower, but then again, it poisons mortals and they do tend to think of themselves as gods."

"Fools, all of them. You could make up anything, call it history, and they'd all believe it. Gaius proved that." I slip the stem into my breast pocket, careful not to kill it. "Your plants are…adequate."

"They're a mockery of the true strength of his power, but you're kind to indulge me, Drayven." The goddess reaches out a hand, smoothing the lapels of my black suit. No one touches Death, and yet she does so brazenly.

"I am not *kind*, Selene. I am here to collect him, not to pay compliments in the name of a god who spent decades in hiding."

"Hiding?" Selene recoils, the word piercing her like an arrow. "He loved it here. This realm was a home to him in a way no other could be. You of all people should understand that."

I turn to face her fully, gripping her elbow and pulling her toward me. I look deep into her eyes, holding her gaze to ensure her attention is fully on me. "Isn't it always what we love that kills us?"

"You tell me," she scoffs. "You are Death. What killed him, Dark One?" Venomous words fall from her too-sweet lips.

"This realm is not capable of sustaining a god and you can feel it. Even the air is harder to breathe here. Gaius separated himself from the sustaining lifeforce of the god realm until it killed him."

The truth. It's raw and ugly, but I feel compelled to give it to her and not the lie the God King is perpetuating throughout the pantheon. He wants every deity to reside in his realm where he has the utmost control over them—and nothing is more dangerous than the idea that they might be able to exist elsewhere, or worse, exist without him.

My hold on her drops as the light in her eyes dims. "Nobus says my father had no worshippers, but when I look around his pyre, all I see are devoted followers. Even if they didn't know who he truly was."

"On that, we agree."

We stand side-by-side, silently observing the mortals paying their respects to the one they call Gavin. My eyes may be on them, but all of my other senses are tuned to her. Just like they always are when the Goddess of Light is near—regardless of how I feel about it.

This realm's single sun inches closer toward the horizon, yet no other deity appears. Not the gods who claimed to be Gaius' friends nor the children he sired.

My hands itch to touch her again, a strange sensation stirring in my chest. I long to comfort the goddess who swallows down the sorrow that leaks from her every pore, but instead, I ball my hands into fists and keep them restrained in the pockets of my onyx trousers.

When the sun finally completes its downward trajectory, the Goddess of Light clears her throat, hurt etched deeply into the lines of her face. "Well, I guess my sisters fell for the lie. I don't know much about funerals, but I know the gifts of Flame and Song would have been welcome additions."

"None of my powers would be of any service to you or I would offer them." I don't know why I say it or why the thought of easing her hurt embedded itself into my demented mind in the first place. Perhaps it's the way she insists on keeping my long forgotten name alive despite my protest. A rare benevolence for the unexplainable comfort it affords me.

"Not now," she states flatly. "Though time would have greatly helped before he died."

"I am not my father. I cannot grant anyone more time nor can I take it away. A few paused moments would not have extended his life by any significant measure. I may be the Reaper of Souls, but I am merely a collector. I do not decide when their time is up."

Selene sighs, her entire body relaxing from her tense posture. "I know. Taura told me it would happen like this; I just didn't want to believe her."

"You shouldn't put your faith in that seer," I rebuke.

"She is not a seer, she is the Goddess of Truth. Her power is just as strong as ours."

"Not as strong as mine," I correct, my voice even-keeled despite the agitation rising in my blood. "You can hide from the truth, but you cannot hide from death."

"That is where you are wrong, Drayven. The truth catches up to everyone eventually. No one can outrun it, even you. Fate will be all of our undoing. Embracing it is the only way we get to actually live."

Selene offers me a final, sad smile. The crowd parts for her without command as she takes her place at the foot of the funeral pyre. Every head bows in solemn reverence for the man they loved.

She takes a torch from an outstretched hand, resorting to man-made fire instead of the magic she had hoped her sister would provide. Words sung in unison begin to rise alongside the flames, an offering from these mortals to the god they didn't know they worshipped.

I linger in the shadows as what remains of Gaius the Green burns. The now-mortal body is engulfed fully as the last light of day vanishes below the horizon. They will stay until nothing but ash remains. *She* will stay.

I admire her humanity, though I do not long for it. Grief is perhaps the cruelest of emotions, and I am grateful that I am incapable of feeling it. To miss someone, to cry for someone, to wait for someone—they are each their own sentence and I am thankful to never be burdened with their pain.

But there is something that burdens me—something that I can't quite name or put my finger on.

Perhaps it's disdain for how Gaius shirked his duty in order to live amongst the mortals who clearly loved him.

Maybe that's why I didn't send one of my Reapers to collect his soul. Maybe that's why I personally arrived days ago when he first passed. Maybe that's why I attended his funeral, and why I stayed by her side all afternoon.

Yes, I like that lie much better than the truth.

CHAPTER 2

DEATH

ONE YEAR LATER

The realm of the gods hasn't changed at all in the last century. The same creatures still fly its skies, the same plants still bloom under its sweltering suns, and the same self-absorbed prick still sits on its throne.

A dull, aching sensation pulls at me as I make my way toward the God King's palace. It's been so long, yet the rough-stitched wound that formed the last time I stepped foot in this realm reeks of festering flesh. I scoff at the absurdity of the comparison. I do not possess a heart, so it's impossible that the nuisance of an organ might rot out from under me.

The grounds are full of deities passing the time outdoors in the near-tropical climate. They lounge on lush green lawns and swim in the pools, all in various states of undress. The God of Revelry holds his own version of court under the willow, lovers and bottles of sweet wine both being passed around under the hanging branches.

Dark magic conceals me as I make my way into the palace. The fewer gods who know about my *summons* the better.

Disgust roils through me at the word.

Nobus has made a show of demanding my presence, mostly to prove that he can order me around, but it's really to brag about the rumored bargain he made with Creation.

The source of life and the all-parent of the gods, Creation does whatever the fuck they please. Whether it's creating a new deity or wiping a realm from existence, the supreme being is at the center of it all. What Nobus bargained for doesn't intrigue me— but how he convinced Creation to make the bargain does. It's the only reason I didn't light his missive on fire and continue my century-long boycott of his realm.

The one and only encounter I've had with Creation ended in a grandiose show of weakness for which I will never forgive myself. One hundred years and the memory still haunts me. Rage and despair, torment and desolation—combinations of feelings that the Dark God of Death should never be subjected to.

A presence prickles the hair on the back of my neck. I peer around the stone corner of the grand palace to find my twin sister at the entrance addressing the sentries standing guard.

How curious.

Nobus' foot soldiers typically patrol the Great Wildes, hunting beasts and keeping the Wolf God's creatures in order, but I've never seen them this close to the palace before.

Tucking that tidbit away for later, I slip past them in the shadows and stalk the marble halls like a predator, searching for anything that might reveal the boon Nobus surely received from Creation.

A century has passed and the bastard hasn't even redecorated. Though, if I'm being honest, a hundred years tends to pass as quickly as one or two these days. Immortality has a nasty habit of making you lose all sense of time. It's the only way we can stomach existing for all eternity.

The hint of a giggle floats across the hall and, instinctively, I move closer to find its source. The Goddess of Light is curled tightly in the bay window that overlooks the grounds. Nestled between pillows, knees hugged tightly to her chest, Selene clutches a worn book. The corner of the page she reads is creased, as if it's been folded and refolded many times, the words meaningful enough to take a permanent place in her heart.

Light from the setting suns filters in through the panes, making the goddess' voluminous blonde curls appear as a glowing cloud of pure sunlight. She reaches into a bowl beside her, plucking red-coated seeds from a fruit and popping them into her mouth as she flips the page, lost completely in her own world.

The aching sensation returns, tugging at the seams of a gaping hole in my chest. What is it like to know contentment like that? To not feel the sharp sting of the past?

Snippets of memories I've long repressed flash in my mind: *cold gray stone, the clicking of a lock, the sting of a whip, the irony tang of blood.*

I slip my hand into my pocket, my fingers wrapping around the single raven feather contained within. On a deep inhale, I let the token ground me to the present. The shadows around me fall away, and for a moment, I consider joining the goddess in the window.

But Death is rarely a welcome companion.

Selene raises a crimson-stained finger to her pink lips, savoring the residual juice with a look of pure bliss. Her eyes flit close as a soft moan, imperceptible to any without immortal hearing, escapes from her. Every muscle in my body stiffens in restraint.

I have watched the goddess from afar for a millennia, always wanting her but never daring to take her. She is too pure to be tainted by my darkness. The scales of the Golden Pantheon only remain balanced when Light and Death sit on opposite sides. Our glances linger, our exchanges turn to banter, but I never act on the burning need that flares to life within me every time I look at the Goddess of Light.

I am a cruel and wicked god, but given the chance, I would gladly be her god.

What wouldn't I give to be the one who elicits that sound from her perfect lips?

"I thought I smelled something rotten." Drayca's irritating voice slices through my fantasy. "What the fuck are you doing here?"

"Your king requested my company, watchdog." I don't hide the ire that coats my words at the sight of her.

War and Death should be the closest friends, eternally sharing offerings and praise. But War is an even crueler god than Death.

Since the dawn of time, mortals have waged war for the most inconsequential of reasons and the outcome is always death. Death of their enemies, death of their kin, or death of their ego— it matters not to me. Either way, death reigns supreme, and that has never sat right with my sister. She is our mother's daughter after all, and the Goddess of Blood was evil incarnate. To make it worse, Drayca helped our mother make me into what I am, sealing both our fates in eternal hatred.

The Goddess of War's white hair, plated intricately into braids of various sizes, falls effortlessly over her broad shoulders. She brushes it aside as she reaches for the axe strapped across her back. "I thought I banished you a century ago."

"I am a king," I reply with authority. "You don't have the power to banish me."

"The king of a realm that should have been mine," she scoffs. "Have you come here to try and steal this one too?"

"Oh come off it, Drayca. You could have killed the cunt and taken it yourself, but you were having too much fun making me bleed."

She rolls the axe handle casually between her pale hands. Her golden eyes burn brighter with each passing minute as she readies her verbal blow. "It's been what? A hundred years since you last tried to pull that *poor, pitiful god* card? Maybe I should cut your fucking head off this time and silence you for good."

I breathe in her hatred, letting the sweet taste flood my senses. "The only *poor, pitiful god* I see here is you. Forever taking orders from Nobus like the bitch you are. The only way you'll ever see the Under Realm is when my magic ends your eternal life."

"Careful, brother." Drayca spits, clearing the bitter taste of the title from her mouth. "Wouldn't want your little doll to hear you speak like that."

Shadows fly up around me, concealing us both from view. My hands find her shoulders and I shove her around the corner and against the stone wall. My forearm presses to her throat in threat. "I don't have a doll and I can speak however the fuck I want. You seem to have forgotten that I am the only one with power great enough to kill a god. Don't provoke me."

"You can lie to yourself all you want, but we both know Light has had a hold over you since the first time you left your tower."

"Dungeon," I correct. "And I paid the price dearly for that escape…or do you forget how she allowed you to cast the final blow?"

"I remember that you didn't come out for a month. Is that why you're still so drawn to the light? Because we deprived you of it?"

A sinister smile pulls at the goddess' lips as she recounts her version of events. To her, I cowered in the darkness, but in truth, it was the first time I traveled to the Under Realm. The day I made the decision that ensured my role as king, forever alone and forever tied to its rules.

My arm drops but I don't step out of Drayca's space. "One day you will cower in the presence of my power. You will pay for your sins with your blood…and I will bathe in it."

A guttural growl vibrates in her chest. "The rules have changed, Dark One, and soon you will find out just how wrong you are."

"Rules?" I chuckle mockingly. "I play by no rules but my own."

Smoke and shadow fill the air between us, the dark magic encasing me as I prepare to disappear. "Tell your master that I will arrive in his chambers when I'm ready."

The sound of steel clanging against stone echoes in the hallway. Without my shadows to muffle the sound of my sister's tantrum, the jarring noise of the axe striking the wall startles the goddess perched casually in the nearby window. Selene stashes the book under the pillows and hurries off with the empty fruit bowl.

I shouldn't pry, but I cannot help myself. Invisible to all, I snatch the book that she held so dearly, slipping it into the space between realms and sending it straight to my study in the Under Realm.

If I cannot have her—body, mind, or soul—I will relish in the things and words that have touched her.

CHAPTER 3

SELENE

"He makes a valid argument, Lyra!"

"Valid or not, it's still dangerous, Nina!"

"Do I want to know where you two are going?" My sisters round the corner of the God King's palace and nearly run headfirst into me. Startled, the color drains from their faces, a stark contrast to the vivid blue and red of their dresses.

"Selene!" Nina clutches her chest, sparks flying from her fingertips as she tries to steady her racing heart and regain control of her power. "You shouldn't lurk in hallways!"

"I wasn't lurking, I was walking. And it's you who should be paying attention when you walk Nobus' halls. Can you imagine if he had stumbled upon you instead of me?"

"*I* wasn't doing anything wrong," Lyra says, her signature smirk pulling up the corner of her lip as she passes me the incriminating paper she holds. "I was simply protecting my sister from making what's sure to be a terrible mistake."

"Somehow I don't quite think Nobus would distinguish between the two."

Those words ring true as I examine the paper. The whisper of a brewing rebellion circulates through the Golden Pantheon, and a time scrawled in the Wolf God's handwriting is proof enough to have both of my sisters exiled.

A fiery spark of a woman, the Goddess of Flame always seems to find herself dangerously close to igniting the darkest desires of those in her company. Mikais is the latest in a long list of the God King's advisors she's become entangled with.

A handler-less operative, she once called herself. Something she picked up from a book she found in one of the countless mortal realms. Nina has spent years whispering in the ears of powerful gods, collecting their secrets and swaying their opinions until she found herself in cahoots with the most ambitious one of all: the Wolf God.

Mikais may be the face of this soon-to-be rebellion, but Nina is his strategist. And if she gets her way, Lyra will be the one singing the battle cry when the war begins.

"Nina—"

My sister holds up her hand, cutting me off. "Don't start with me, Selene."

"Unless you want to finally admit your terrible taste in males, too, of course," Lyra adds. Her eyes sparkle as she speaks, the cadence of her voice slipping into the sing-songy tone she uses to lure mortals to do her bidding—a tone that has no effect on me.

"I have never been romantically involved with anyone trying to lead a…a…" I look around to make sure no one lingers in the hallways before leaning in and whispering the words that would find me beside the goddesses at their exile. "A rebellion."

"I am not romantically involved with him, and it is not a rebellion. It's a change in leadership," Nina corrects.

"It's treason! Whatever part you're considering playing in Mikais' ludicrous plan, I suggest you change your mind, quickly."

My sister's eyes burn, embers of rage and hatred evident in the smouldering irises of the Goddess of Flame. It takes only a fraction of a second for me to realize that my words fall on deaf ears.

We have all suffered under Nobus' cruel rule, but the defamation of our father was the final straw for Nina. Each of us dealt with the grief of losing him differently. I threw a funeral, but Nina helped start a rebellion. She wants to see the God King burn and doesn't care who carries the torch. Mikais and his little power grab are simply convenient timing.

I can't help but wonder if Lyra is more involved in Nina's plans than she claims. Has the Goddess of Song used her powers to coerce the Wolf God? Or does his hatred and disloyalty to his brother stem from something else entirely?

"This is happening whether you like it or not, Selene. I suggest you see the error in your refusal before you find yourself on the wrong side of history."

Nina storms off in a blaze of fury, Lyra following closely at her heels. The paper in my hand turns to ash as my sisters depart.

"It's always the youngest siblings that are the spitfires."

The sensual, disembodied voice stirs something in me as I scan my surroundings for the corporeal form of its owner. A swirling mass of shadows appears in the white-washed hallway, the toes of his polished shoes coming into view atop the gold-veined marble floors. I follow them upwards as the god I last saw over a year ago slowly appears in front of me.

"You shouldn't eavesdrop," I chastise as the wisps part to reveal Drayven's chiseled face.

"You shouldn't discuss rebellion in the palace of the king you plan to overthrow."

With a snap of my fingers, I extinguish the lights that line the hallway, casting us into total darkness. A quick deterrent to anyone who may be wandering nearby. There's nothing to see—and more importantly, nothing to hear—in this hallway.

"Do you want me *dead?*" I whisper through clenched teeth.

"Nobus will send me to the Under Realm faster than you can say the word 'go.'"

A cool chuckle echoes in the dark. "You would hate it there."

He's wrong. I can't say for certain how I know, but I feel it in my bones. The dark depths of the Under Realm crave the light, and I wonder if he can feel it too.

"Do you hate it there?"

The lack of light emboldens me to ask the question that has plagued me ever since I saw him that night more than a century ago. The Dark God on his knees in the slate that covers the beach, hands tangled in his ghostly hair, green eyes shining in the light from the crescent moons.

I watched him from behind the boulders that line the shore, listened as sobs wracked his body. As the first sun rose to chase the moons from the sky, Death removed his shirt, soaked with the salty evidence of his blood-mixed tears, and disappeared in a swirling mass of onyx night.

Silence envelops us as it becomes clear he isn't going to answer. I take a step forward in the darkness, certain I will discover that I'm now alone.

Strong hands grip my shoulders, stopping me as my nose grazes his stone chest. Cold emanates from him, my skin turning to ice everywhere he touches. A shiver snakes up my spine and he drops his hold.

"I will ask you the same." His tone is as cold as his touch. "If you join Mikais, you'll never be allowed here again. There is no telling which realm he will exile you to, but Nobus will pick one that will destroy you slowly. So ask yourself, Selene. Do *you* hate it *here*?"

"You do." It's not a question, but a declaration.

Drayven didn't step foot in the God Realm for a hundred years after that night. Rumors have flown wildly amongst the gods, but I alone know the truth: something or someone here hurt him terribly.

"What are you even doing here?"

"I was summoned." The agitation is clear in his clipped voice.

"Kings can be summoned? I thought royalty simply did as they pleased."

"I only do things that please me." Drayven's breath tickles my cheek as he speaks. "Nobus thinks he's flexing his power, but I know something he doesn't. His little princeling is arriving tomorrow, and what better threat than for Death to attend the birth."

"You wouldn't steal his heir. You aren't cruel."

"I am cruel, Light, and you would do well to remember that." His voice booms over my head again, the god no longer crowding my space. "I won't steal his heir, but the prince will come willingly to my realm one day. He will be drawn to its darkness."

"You speak of your home as if it is nothing but brokenness and despair. That can't possibly be all there is."

"It is," he counters curtly.

"It is not, and I can prove it." Silence settles between us again. He doesn't move, doesn't speak, doesn't even breathe. This time I am positive that the god has disappeared, but I whisper my plea anyway. "Give me one day there."

"No." The single word spoken in the abyss rattles my bones.

Seems he has not left after all, and it's that thought, that curiosity, that pushes me further. "Are you afraid of being wrong, Dark One?"

"Hardly," he says with a chuckle, the sound sending an errant shiver down my spine again. "It's you who should be afraid. The Under Realm is no place for your light."

It's my turn to chuckle. "You have made a very big mistake, Your Majesty. You see, I am a stubborn god and you have just challenged me. Now I must go to the Under Realm and I will not rest until you agree. You would save yourself a world of trouble by just saying 'yes.'"

He is close enough that I feel his chest rumble as he growls.

"I will wear you down eventually," I declare, reaching out to lay my palm against the hard plane of his chest. "That's the thing about being immortal. We have nothing but time, Drayven."

"Do not call me that." His hand wraps around my wrist, yanking it from where it rests. "I am Death and you will address me as such." His eyes, now narrowed to snake-like slits, glow in the darkness.

My voice slips into the familiar timbre of authority. The imbalance of power in this dynamic does not swing in his favor, and he will know that without question. "I am the Goddess of Light. What thrives in the dark cowers from me."

In a blinding flash, the lights return to their full intensity. Drayven drops my hand to shield his eyes from the light—*my light*. His shadows wrap around him instinctively and I can't resist reaching a hand through their mist. They tingle, making the hairs on my arm stand to attention, but they do not harm me.

"Hmm," I muse as the shadows shirk from the golden light that pours from my body. "I will illuminate your realm and you will see what has been right in front of you all along."

A world full of endless night must contain moonlight and starlight. One step into his realm and I could show him the beauty in the darkness. Constellations and auroras, shooting stars in the fabric of his sky—all of which would steal his breath. I know they exist. I feel them calling to me even here.

He steps closer, forcing me to look up at him. "You intrigue me. There is something about you…" Drayven lifts my chin, tilting it to one side and then the other slowly. "Hmm," he ponders.

"What?" I ask in a whisper.

"You see something where there is nothing." His fingers trail down the center of my throat. I hold my breath through their agonizingly slow descent until they rest atop the hollow of my neck. "It will be your demise."

"I am not afraid of you." I declare the truth boldly. It's not the god who scares me, but the hunger I've felt in his presence for hundreds of years. And it nearly brings me to my knees.

"Oh, but you should be, Light." Drayven bends down, his breath brushing the shell of my ear as he speaks. "You should be very afraid."

The Dark God of Death steps back letting his shadows conceal him once again. Before the last wisps of his magic vanish from sight, one final whisper fills the hall. "Try to stay out of trouble, goddess."

CHAPTER 4

SELENE

One year later

"Why does it have to be in his bedroom?"

I stare up at the obsidian and red carvings that cover the gaudy door. Unlike the others in the palace depicting beautiful scenes of the creatures that inhabit our myriad of realms, the Wolf God demanded the rose quartz sculptures on his bedroom door be replaced with this visual atrocity. Mikais has been accused of many things in his eternal life, but no one has ever accused him of having taste.

"For the last time, it's a meeting not an orgy," Nina sighs.

"An orgy would be preferable. Significantly lower chance of being exiled." I roll my eyes as Nina taps a series of coded knocks on the door.

An entire year of her going on and on about how imperative it is that I listen to Mikais' proposal has landed me in this moment. Despite my protests that I am only here to listen, there will be no going back once I cross the threshold.

No one has seen Arcasia since she gave birth to the prince. Rumors of her imprisonment and Nobus' dominance over his wife and child circulate through the pantheon, further accelerating the growing movement to dethrone him.

Something about the baby terrifies the God King, and he's waiting until the prince's birthday and the bestowing of blessings to decide if he will live or die—an act that I cannot stomach no matter how much I may wish to avoid Mikais' war.

Coded knocks respond to Nina's petition. Taura stands in the now open doorway, her raven hair pinned atop her head, blue eyes shifting to violet when she sees me.

"I told you she'd come," the Goddess of Truth smiles over her shoulder. "And I am never wrong."

"Selene has finally decided to join us, has she? Welcome to the rebellion." Mikais greets us with open arms. I step to the side, avoiding the hug he seems primed to give.

The inside of the god's room is exactly how I imagined someone with his proclivities would decorate. A giant four-poster bed spans the width of the room. At least eight deities lounge on the silver silk bedding, all dressed, thank Creation. Bottles of chilled wine rest on low tables next to crystal flutes, trays of fruit, and half-burned candles.

It might not be an orgy yet, but the room is certainly prepared for one.

I give the bed a wide berth as I make my way towards the floor-to-ceiling window that faces the mountains. The two suns cast the room in an eerie, purple haze as they descend below the range.

Even within the walls of the palace, my power can feel the moons that hover just out of view, calling to take their rightful place in the night sky. I yearn to give them what they long for, to flex the power that grows more restless with each day.

"I thought I told you to stay out of trouble."

I turn my attention toward the black-clad god lounging atop a pile of silver pillows. Legs outstretched, arms behind his head, and white hair mussed, Drayven looks more at ease than I've ever seen him.

"That's your fault for thinking I'd listen to you." I smile playfully.

"What are you doing here, Selene?"

"The better question is 'what are you doing here,' oh Dark One? Answering another royal summons?"

"Hardly," he scoffs. "My presence is unwanted, which is exactly how I prefer it."

"Well…if I wasn't already curious about this rebellion, consider me intrigued now."

"You shouldn't be." Drayven's green eyes narrow, his demeanor shifting to something unreadable. "You should stay out of this, Light."

I should, but I won't. The kindling has been laid and the Golden Pantheon will be fully aflame soon. Siding with Mikais might mean certain exile, but a comfortable existence will never be worth siding with a king whose sole concern is power. A king so concerned with it that he would willingly murder his own child.

Eager to redirect the conversation, I pick up the red fruit from a nearby tray and toss it his way. "Here."

A hand made entirely of dark magic shoots out and catches the fruit inches from his face. "What is this?"

"It's called a pomegranate. An interesting little food I discovered on my travels. It's filled with the most delicious seeds."

Something unreadable sparks in Drayven's eyes, there one second and gone the next.

"Why do I need a pomegranate?" he asks, turning the red orb over in his pale hand, the silver rings adorning his fingers pressing into the fruit's flesh.

"It'll give you something to occupy yourself with instead of worrying about me." I smile sweetly, beaming at the scathing look the Dark God shoots my way.

"Someone has to worry about you. You clearly possess no self-preservational instincts. Joining rebellions, begging to go to the Under Realm…"

"Gods don't beg. And going to the Under Realm *is* self-preservation," I correct.

"Is it now?"

"It is. I need a single day to make your realm shine. And all of that new light…well, that would feed my power immensely." I bend down, swatting at his black boots until he sits up. Taking their place on the silver pillows, I lay back, imitating his former pose. "One day, Dark One, and my hunger would be satisfied."

"It's not your hunger I worry about, Light."

Drayven cracks open the fruit and lifts the rind to his mouth. He drinks deep, sucking down the tart liquid. When he pulls back, a single drop of blood red juice leaks from the corner of his lips. Green eyes lock onto mine as his pale thumb slowly swipes it away, the silver ring on his finger sparkling in the purple light.

The sudden urge to lean in and taste it overtakes me, and I feel my teeth sink into my bottom lip.

Mikais clears his throat and every god in the room turns their attention to him. Every god except Drayven. I feel his eyes bore into me as the Wolf God speaks, but I don't meet them again.

"Let's get down to business. As you know, Nobus has demanded our presence two nights from now." A groan resounds in the space, its source unknown but its meaning echoed by all. "I know, I know. I am usually a fan of the elaborate parties my brother forces us to attend in his honor, but I don't relish in celebrating the birthday of his little princeling any more than you do."

"Be that as it may, the required bestowing of blessings to the Prince of the Gods affords us an opportunity that we cannot pass up." Nina's red hair glows as she joins in sharing the plan that she clearly influenced. "While we are on bended knee and every eye is trained on the little heir, we will put phase one into motion."

"The attendance of every god is required at the ceremony," Mikais continues. "Every god but one."

The god beside me tenses. Shadows hover in my peripheral as every eye turns in our direction. I sit up, spine stiffening in preparation for Mikais' next words.

"Once we have given our gifts to the child, Death will make his grand entrance."

Murmurs fill the room, their faces ranging from delight to disgust. Drayven, ever stoic, doesn't speak. Something unexpected bubbles up inside of me, something I can't tamper down quickly enough. The sconces on the wall illuminate unexpectedly, the conspiring gods flinching as their eyes adjust.

Nina glares at me, a nasty rebuke forming on her tongue, but I cut her off before she has the chance to voice it. "If we harm the child, we are no better than Nobus."

"I would never harm a child, Selene." Mikais laughs off my concern, the rest of the gods joining him. "We have much bigger plans for him."

Bigger plans. Nausea rolls in my gut.

Taura looks at me, her eyes shifting hues again, and I know she's reading a truth. She lets out a sigh and nods, silently confirming the Wolf God's words. They will not physically harm him, at least not yet.

He is a baby, a prince, and yet he is nothing more than a pawn to them. The Prince of the Gods has a powerful role to play in this game—and these gods plan to use him as leverage against his father.

"Consider what will be necessary for our young prince to be successful and craft your blessings appropriately. Remember, my brother shouldn't be aware of the weapon we are creating until Death appears."

Weapon. The word lingers heavily in the air.

"Still want to join us?" Drayven asks as the other gods go back to their conversations, each theorizing the ways they might word their gifts.

"At what point do we become worse than Nobus?" I ask. "Are we simply the lesser of the inevitable evils? Are we so far removed from humanity that we've forgotten how to be good?"

"Gods do not have humanity. We were made from the raw matter of Creation, not of the fragile fabric of mortality. Eternal life is not our gift; it is our curse. And to be eternal, you must be ruthless."

"And what if I wish to be something else?" The whispered question pains me to say aloud.

Shadows form around the dark god as he starts to fade from view. "Then I would be very, very clear with the blessing you bestow."

CHAPTER 5

SELENE

Every corner of Nobus' palace is decorated for the event. From the foyer of the grand entrance to the golden throne room, every surface drips with opulence. Gods from across the pantheon were ordered to the palace days ago to begin the preparations, offering their gifts to ensure a celebration fit for a king.

But only time will tell which king we celebrate. Will it be the vengeful one that sits the throne now, the babe in line to take his place, or the wolf plotting rebellion?

All eyes are on the dais as the royal family makes their way from behind the curtain that conceals the entrance to their chambers. From his towering height to his broad build, Nobus' presence commands attention—so much so that it would be easy not to notice the dark-haired goddess who sulks in his shadow.

Downtrodden, there is no spark in Arcasia's gray eyes, only the blank expression of someone who would rather be anywhere else than here. Unlike her husband, the goddess' presence has waned during her seclusion. Whispers flit between the gods as we catch our first glimpse of the goddess in two years.

The orchestra's song reaches a crescendo as Nobus jerks the swaddled babe from the Goddess of Protection's arms and raises him over his head. All heads bow and knees bend in the presence of the young prince.

Peering up from under my lashes, I sneak a glimpse at the child and instantly understand why the king has kept him hidden for the first year of his life.

The child held aloft in front of kneeling gods has hair as dark as night and glimmering gray eyes—traits entirely from his mother and not from the supposedly all-powerful deity who sired him.

It is a rare trait for a god's eyes to not be the signature golden hue of our pantheon's namesake, and those gods are always fated for something tremendous. It's widely believed that Arcasia's eyes destined her to be our queen, much in the same way Drayven's determined his right to rule the Under Realm over his twin sister, Drayca.

If the son of Nobus does not have his father's eyes, then the target on his back is even greater than we realized.

"Arise and offer your powers to Calaedon, Prince of the Gods."

"Lyra." I turn to my sister, grabbing her arm as she moves to enter the queue of deities that line up to grant seeds of their magic to the child. "He's going to absorb—"

"Shhh!" My sister places her palm over my mouth and pulls me towards her. "Don't you think we know that?" she hisses in my ear. "Why do you think I finally gave into Nina's pleas and joined her?"

Lyra swipes my pink lipstick off her hand as she joins the other gods. The few I know to be rebellion members are spaced purposefully throughout the line, no two back-to-back to ensure Nobus doesn't recognize the pattern hidden in the blessings.

The Wolf God approaches the dais first. "To my nephew, I gift the mouth of the wolf. May your words always be commands, may your teeth always be sharp, and may your bite always crush your foes."

Nobus beams with pride, nodding in appreciation at the blessing he thinks is complete.

"And I also gift the eyes of the lamb. May your eyes always reflect the content of your heart and may they always see the true intentions of those you look upon."

The God King tenses as Mikais finishes. The young prince absorbs the golden embers of power given freely to him, the cradle he rests in glowing momentarily as the magic settles.

The duality of the offering—all at once something Nobus both wants and rejects—sets the tone for what's expected of the rest of the rebels.

One by one, the powerful kneel in front of the royal family. From bended knee, they each bestow a single present meant to aid the prince in his life and hinder the king if he takes it by force.

Nobus' golden eyes shine with envy at the offerings, already counting the ways his power will increase once he slaughters his own son.

Lyra steps to the dais next, the sapphire taffeta of her gown rippling like waves down the steps as she kneels. "To the prince, I gift the song of destiny. May fate know him by the sound of his name."

Nobus doesn't hide his scoff. On the surface, it's a sweet gift—one that a child soon to die has no need of. But my sister is smarter than that. Her blessing ensures that fate, and whatever it might have in store for him, can find the prince no matter which realm he's in.

With each gift, the child glows more intensely until he outshines the suns themselves. The perfect timing for my own gift.

Like my sister, I do not prepare him to die, but instead amplify her blessing even more. No matter what happens, the gods will always be able to find him.

"To the prince," I start, my heart hammering in my chest as I try to steady my breathing. "May the light surround you so that you will always be recognized by your kind."

Like a beacon in the night, a lighthouse on the coast, or an angel in the darkness, no matter where this war leads, no matter where this child ends up, those with magic in their blood will always know him by his halo of light.

My hands tremble as I descend and meld into the crowd again.

Drayca ascends next, bestowing a gift that causes Nobus to swell with pride at the most envious blessing yet—the gift of strategy. "May he always know the path to victory."

Nina bestows the gift of the flame, placing the fire of passion in his blood.

Bastin grants the ability to satisfy every lover, a gift that earns him a glare from both monarchs. The God of Revelry, who has chosen to side with Nobus, is either oblivious to the God King's plan or is publicly insulting his abilities in the bedroom. Either way, it makes for great entertainment—which is one of his specialties.

The Goddess of the Harvest grants the gift of a bountiful table, a gift the king cannot fathom the necessity of. But Seblee isn't a fool. Abundance reigns in this realm, but many of the others are deficient. The ability to never be without is a true gift.

When the last divine blessing has been bestowed upon the child, Nobus signals for Taura to approach. She kneels at the feet of the God King, her violet eyes shifting hues as she takes the prince's tiny, glowing hand into hers.

The Goddess of Truth is an expert liar. She is skilled at keeping her face neutral, but I know her tells. The way one muscle in her jaw tightens slightly, the way her lashes flutter four times—all signs that the truth she sees isn't palatable.

"His future is blurry, my King. So much is yet to be determined."

"Unacceptable," Nobus roars. "Tell me what you see or you will never see again." Lightning ripples across his skin as his power rumbles through the palace.

Taura cuts her eyes to me quickly and my heart drops into my stomach. Whatever she truly sees involves me, and I have no doubt revealing this vision would end us both. The goddess takes a steadying breath, preparing to only give away the most crucial pieces of information while tucking the details safely away.

"The very sight of him will cause men to cower, Your Majesty. He will be….he will be…"

The lights in the throne room flicker as Taura searches for words that won't find her exiled. Black smoke fills the space and all attention shifts to the spinning, tornadic shadows that concentrate at the foot of the dais.

His voice booms through the dark before his corporeal form appears. "Quite the gathering you're hosting, Nobus. I do hope I haven't missed all the fun."

The Dark God of Death melds into view, moving towards the baby that glows in the golden cradle.

"You will not touch him," Arcasia growls, a hint of her fabled beast form coming to the surface.

"Calm down, beast," Drayven scolds. "I will not touch your child and I will not curse him either. But I will tell you what Truth is too afraid to say."

Taura stands, backing away from the kings who now stand toe-to-toe, each poised to unleash their deadly wrath at any moment.

"Your son will be forged in battle, molded in blood, and crowned in shadows."

A gasp ripples through the crowd. Nobus raises a hand to strike but the dark god disappears in a flash of black. Thunder claps and Drayven reappears against the back wall. He lounges with casual ease, swiping something invisible from the shoulder of his black dress suit.

"How dare you threaten your prince!" the God King roars.

"He's not *my* prince. It is not a threat; it is the truth. Tell him, Taura."

All attention turns to the raven-haired goddess who trembles slightly at my side. "It is as he says, my King," she whispers.

Nobus stiffens, emotions warring in his golden gaze before a wicked smile blooms on his face.

"Well." He chuckles. "It seems even the Under Realm will bow. A ruler who wears two crowns. What father wouldn't be proud of that?"

His sinister tone makes the hair stand on my arms. Whatever half-truth Drayven chose to share, he has spared the child for now.

But as Taura has told me many times, fate is not written in stone; it is written in the shifting sands of time.

Nobus will keep the boy alive until he is able to determine how to change the fate proclaimed here today as truth. He will focus on the dark god and spend his days plotting how to overthrow the king of the Under Realm, biding his time until the little princeling has enough power to take the dark throne.

And if his attention is on Drayven, it won't be on Mikais.

CHAPTER 6

SELENE

No one parties like a god— especially when the party is orchestrated by the God of Revelry himself.

Wine sweeter than nectar flows freely from the tiered fountain in the center of the courtyard where the afterparty is in full swing. Poured from too-full goblets into open mouths, tongues lap and lips caress as the intoxicating liquid is passed from god to god.

The air smells of fruit and sins of the flesh. Half-dressed deities dance wildly under the light of the full moons, swaying in near trance-like states to the melodic swell of the orchestra. Strings, horns, and woodwinds play in perfect harmony as the Goddess of Song serenades the partygoers, her melody releasing the last of their inhibitions.

Bastin's power grows with every offering, and the post-ceremony party will only descend deeper into debauchery as the night stretches on. What remains of their clothing will soon be shed and their partners will soon be shared. More gods will flex their magic, driving them all further into madness and pleasure.

Every god seeks one thing tonight: escape.

Escape from their duties and from the war that brews around them. They have no aim but to be lost so thoroughly that only the rising sun can lead them home again.

I wander through the moonlit gardens, letting my fingers trail across the delicate petals of the blooming flowers in search of my own escape. The party doesn't interest me, but the god lingering at the edge of the hedge maze does. Funny how I seem to always be able to find him, even in the darkness he loves to cling to.

"That was some show you put on." I smile, but Drayven doesn't acknowledge me. He broods, silently surrounded by his comforting shadows as he stares off at the horizon.

"You knew." My statement comes out like an accusation. "You knew about the prince's eyes and that's why you sided with the Wolf."

Drayven finally directs his attention to me, the full weight of his cold gaze nearly knocking the breath from my lungs.

"Stop," he commands. Pushing off the hedge he reclines against, the dark god stands to his full height. "Stop trying to see something in me that does not exist."

"I'm not trying to do anything. I am simply stating a fact."

"You want facts, Selene?" Drayven steps forward, his large hand gripping me forcefully by the chin. The silver rings adorning his fingers press into my skin. "The Wolf promises me offerings. I do not care about the child or who sits that cursed throne. I am here to collect the souls of dead gods, nothing more."

"Liar." I spit the word at him. "You care what happens to him because his fate is tied to you."

"You don't know what you're talking about," he grits through clenched teeth.

"Then tell me." I shove him backward, his hand dropping from my face as he stumbles a single step in surprise before regaining his footing. "Tell me what Taura told you."

"No. It's my curse to bear."

"It involves me and I know it!" My skin glows white as my temper flares. "I saw it in her eyes."

"You have no idea what you saw," the dark god growls. "Drop it, Light."

Power boils in my veins as I try and fail to control the rage that filters through me. For too long my light has been seen as naivety, as goodness and sunshine. But I am also the moon, and the stars, and the illumination from blistering, burning fires. I am the electric tingle of lightning in the storm and the light that blinds you as your life ends.

I am a goddess of the Golden Pantheon—and I am tired of being discounted.

"Do you think you are untouchable, Dark One?" I step forward, invading his space and forcing him backward. "Do you think you are the only god powerful enough to change the course of this rebellion? You have seen what I am capable of, and yet you still think I am weak." My finger digs into his granite chest as I press on. "Your darkness cannot exist without my balance and it is time you see me as the equal I am."

Drayven grips my wrist. Pulling my hand back, he lifts it towards his face, examining the still pointed finger. His green eyes lock onto mine as a devilish smirk pulls up the corner of his mouth.

"Careful, Light. Bastin's magic stokes all manners of desires tonight. I wouldn't provoke me, if I were you."

I rip my hand from his grasp and shove him again. "I do not start what I cannot win."

In a flash of black, the Dark God vanishes. He reappears behind me, spinning me until my back presses into the hedges. "Is that so?" Drayven leans down, the tip of his nose grazing the side of my face as he speaks low into my ear. "What exactly are you hoping to win?"

White tendrils of his hair brush across my face as he pulls back.

Hovering inches away, Death's breath is hot on my face. I should cower from the sparkling emeralds that peer into my soul. I should fear the villainous features and malevolent body that crowd my space. But all they do is stoke the fire burning within me that emboldens me further.

"A bargain," I say with renewed fervor. "Grant me a day in the Under Realm and I won't ask you about the vision again."

He shakes his head vigorously. Whether to convince me or himself, I cannot be sure.

"Only a fool makes a bargain with Death."

"You have always thought I was a fool. Make the deal and find out once and for all if you're right."

Drayven's chuckle reverberates through me as he scans my face. My words tempt him, and I pounce on the chance to further goad him into accepting my bargain. Calling to my power, I dial up the intensity of my eyes until the golden irises shimmer like flames.

"You want to say yes," I taunt seductively.

His breath hitches as my fiery gaze sucks him deeper into my orbit. Instinctively, the Dark God leans impossibly closer. I swallow down the chill that dances across my skin as his icy lips lightly graze the tips of mine.

"What I want is not important," he breathes.

Heat pools in my core, my own breath catching in my chest as I fight the urge to meet his advance.

There has always been something between us, some hint of chemistry, some ember of desire easily written off as witty banter or snarky comebacks, but there has never been anything so outright as this.

Perhaps it is Bastin's power or Lyra's song— or perhaps they are convenient excuses for something that has been brewing for a millenia.

"Accept the deal." My whispered words kiss his lips. "Take me to the Under Realm, Drayven."

The Dark God's eyes shutter at the sound of his true name. He swallows reflexively and I sense the moment he knows he can no longer resist me.

"You will regret this, Light."

Drayven pulls me into his arms, his lips crushing mine as an obsidian mass of swirling night envelopes us. Thunder booms and the garden of gods fades into nothingness.

His tongue dips into my mouth as the pull of gravity releases us. I am afloat in the ether between realms and he is my tether, my charted course to a forbidden destination. He angles my head to drink me in deeper, his fingers tightening in my golden hair.

We fall through space and time, tangled endlessly in each other. I feel his strong arms under my thighs as he cradles my body against his chest and finally breaks our kiss.

"You will hate me after this."

My eyes pop open at his words and, for the first time, I take in the Under Realm.

CHAPTER 7

SELENE

My fingers trail across the bare, white walls. Bone, stripped of its flesh and bleached, is smoother than I thought it would be.

I try to steady my breathing as I take in the sights of Death's study—the mahogany desk, the vase of deep purple flowers atop it, the leather chair that matches the black marble floors.

The fire roaring in the hearth does little to warm the room but it looks pretty, especially with the way the emerald eyes of the onyx serpents adorning the mantle sparkle in its flames. I move closer to it, willing it to be a distraction from the heady rush of magic washing through me.

To the naked eye, there is little light here, but I sense it in everything. The obsidian sky, visible through the domed glass ceiling overhead, screams for my attention. Thousands of tiny, invisible stars hide in its endless dark, each one beckoning me to uncover their light.

But these stars feel *wrong*. They are unlike any light I've encountered before. Every part of me screams to unleash the full force of my magic, to release them from their eternal cages and permit them to ascend, but I resist. Acting on instinct is a surefire way to find myself back in Nobus' realm before I've satisfied my curiosity. Before I've shown the Dark God of Death what truly lurks in his shadows.

"You're trembling." Drayven's voice is as cold as the room. His back is to me as he pours two glasses of amber liquid from a crystal decanter. "This should calm your nerves."

He turns to hand me a glass and I force my face to remain neutral at the sight of the changed deity before me. The hulking mass of the Dark God stalks toward me, his green eyes glowing eerily in the firelight. Black tattoos spider across his hands and neck, crawling and twisting in sharp contrast to the ethereal sheen of his porcelain skin.

Drayven sets the glasses on the desk and removes his jacket. He rolls the sleeves of his shirt, slowly revealing more of the dark magic that decorates every inch of skin.

"Welcome to my home." The Dark God smiles sadly, exposing the points of his now enlongated canines. Teeth designed to shred flesh in a single bite. "Things are different here, Selene."

The way he tenses on the word *different* tells me all I need to know about how he interprets his appearance in his realm—how he expects me to interpret it.

I step toward him and trace the lines of ink on his forearm with my index finger. They retract from my touch at first before slithering inquisitively toward me.

"I like different."

My eyes lock onto his and I feel the full weight of his piercing gaze—a gaze said to read the full measure of a soul in a single glance before passing judgement.

But the eyes staring back to me do not weigh if I should reside in the Fiery Lakes or the Eternal Meadows. These eyes are frozen, unreadable except for the tiniest spark of hope around the edges of his irises.

"Hold your judgment until you've seen my realm." Drayven lifts the glass of amber liquid to his mouth, his rings tapping gently against the crystal as he moves.

I follow his lead, letting the whiskey warm me as it flows down my throat. "Show it to me, then. Show me your darkest night and I will show you the light."

He shakes his head, scoffing softly as he takes the empty glass from my hand. "Confident, aren't we, goddess?"

Drayven plants both hands on my shoulders as his shadows begin to swirl around us again. "You will find that there is only darkness here."

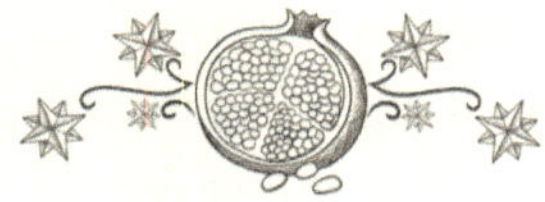

I feel the wispy bands of his magic disappear. They fade into the tenebrous ether that surrounds us outside the confines of his study. Drayven's hands slide down my arms, gripping my biceps to steady me in the void.

To him, this is infinite darkness. To me, this is merely an eclipse. Not everlasting, but a momentary umbra. My knees nearly buckle under the weight of possibility. This is not a directionless abyss. It is a blank canvas aching to be painted in ultraviolet light.

Drayven's thumbs rub circles on my skin, mistaking my quivering restraint for fear. His breath is hot against my ear as he speaks. "Whatever you expected to find, it's not here."

"Yes it is." My words fly out in a hushed, hurried whisper as raw magic floods my veins. It's one thing to see the darkness through glass and another to stand in it, to feel it in every crevice of my being.

The sharp inhalation of breath shreds my lungs, my entire body quaking as the veiled stars reach a screaming crescendo. The sound of my scream rips through the pitch black as magic pours from my body with my exhale.

Dazzling rivulets of gold blaze across the obsidian sky, my power dancing through the fabric of the Under Realm. Spiraling gilded bands of light leapfrog across the night, illuminating the once-hidden stars. Blinding constellations now shine brilliantly against the inky backdrop.

"Selene." My name sounds like a prayer as it falls from his lips.

Another wave of magic washes through me as more stars join in the symphony that begs for my light. I throw my head back as a sparkling column of magic erupts from my open mouth.

My entire body vibrates with power, somehow too much and yet not enough. I loosen every hold, unchain every restraint, as I reshape the Under Realm.

Drayven's hands move to cradle the sides of my face and that's when I feel it — the effects of what I've uncovered.

The blazing comets and shining orbs aren't stars, but souls. Desperate, hungry souls searching for a way out of the eternal night.

His power is like ice, but it does little to cool my burning skin. Magic encases us as we lose ourselves in the intoxicating rush of our duties.

We work in tandem, lost in our own power. I light the path and the King of the Under Realm, the Reaper of Souls, and the Lord of Darkness shepherds them to their eternal home.

With each passing moment, our bodies inch impossibly closer. My breaths turn to pants as my blood heats. I bite my lip, absent-mindedly rubbing my thighs together.

Light courses through me, unfettered and unmoored, incinerating my control. I am lost in the haze of immortal power, captivated by the forbidden god who holds me, and desperate for release.

My hand trails between us, my fingers eager to provide what I seek. Drayven's hands slide from my face, tracing every curve on their descent to stop my needy fingers. His touch is cold as he pulls my hand away from my body.

My eyes fly open, locking onto his, my own spark of need reflected as he takes a step back.

A large, ornately carved chair appears behind him. A stunning ivory moth is inlaid in the ebony wood, its long hindwing tails trailing from the sigil to frame the monarch's head. All-seeing eyes of sparkling emerald adorn the four grand wings. The King of the Under Realm sits on his throne in a single, fluid motion, his hungry eyes never leaving mine.

With one crook of his fingers, he motions me forward. Lifting the golden silk of my gown, I crawl over him, dropping to one knee at a time as I slowly straddle the Dark God.

He grips my hips, his strong fingers digging into my soft flesh so hard a mortal would bruise. Drayven tugs me closer, my hips rolling over the hard press of him as he nips at my ear.

"Use me."

Two words. A plea or a command, it matters not. The magic that brought me to this point still rages in my veins, still screams at me to use more until both my power and my body are spent.

I move against him, writhing in his lap as power floods out of me in golden waves. More and more of the endless chasm of black yields to my light.

Drayven never moves, the pressure of his grip never loosening as he holds me flush against him.

His magical tattoos, however, have different plans. They jump from the Dark God's skin, forming vines to wrap around my limbs and rove over every inch of my body. Inky tendrils dip into my bodice, caressing my breasts and plucking my nipples. I moan at the welcome intrusion, further emboldening them. The thick vines wrapping around the tops of my thighs slip further under my bunched dress, exploring my aching, slick skin.

But still I need more.

I feel the fabric of the Under Realm split—not much, but enough that the deity currently pinning me to his lap should be concerned. I open my eyes to take in the glittering, iridescent aurora. Glowing streaks of green and purple tint the white waves of the Dark God's hair, but it's hunger that colors his expression.

Drayven's dark magic surges upward, the tattoos stroking my clit and teasing at my entrance as he urges me closer to oblivion. Swollen and sensitive, I rush headfirst into delicious release as his lips find my neck. The sharp points of his teeth scrape against my flesh as he drags his tongue slowly up the column of my throat, tasting the residual power on my skin.

I am breathless and wanton, shaking on the lap of the King of the Under Realm as reality settles in. This is what I wanted—to uncover the light, to shape and mold the darkness, to remake it and feed my power. And while what we just did wasn't planned, it's been brewing for a millenia.

Drayven releases my hips, his tattoos return to their place on his skin, and I brace for him to lash out and send me away for destroying his home.

"And to think..." He smirks. "I haven't even shown you the darkest parts of my world yet."

My mouth hangs agape at the reaction I didn't expect. "You want to show me more?" I ask in disbelief.

Drayven rubs his jaw, the silver rings reflecting the light of my aurora as his lips lift into a predatory smile. "I will show you every unlit corner of my realm under one condition. The next time you come, it will be on my cock."

CHAPTER 8

SELENE

The deeper we travel into the Under Realm, the more I'm certain Drayven expected me to run away screaming. But I don't. The abysmal dark that permeates his realm only makes my power stronger.

I use a little here and there, but nothing elicits the same reaction, the same need from me that bloomed when I uncovered the veiled souls.

The grand slate staircase that descends from the King's palace is now adorned with a starry runner of light. The boatman who ferries the dead across the blood rivers now has a shining, eternally lit lantern. No corner of this land will be without a touch of my power soon.

Drayven's hold on my hand tightens as we near the Fiery Lakes, but the screams of the damned souls don't frighten me. His power heightens here, surrounded by wickedness. I lean into it as I let my own magic out to play. Soon, the fires blaze brighter and the wailing howls of the dead intensify under the scorching flames.

To a mortal, we are sinful, devious and villainous, for how we relish in the sound. But we are gods—and gods have no real moral compass, only the need to temporarily satiate an unquenchable thirst for power and control.

I breathe in the sulfuric air and use my light in the most iniquitous way yet. Golden power ripples out of me in waves as a blacklit canopy of constellations forms overhead. The star-structures look different for each soul. Instead of pictures of gods, they depict the greatest of each soul's sins, replaying the acts that sentenced them to eternal fire on a constant loop.

Drayven's pallid skin sparkles under the dazzling celestial sky as he swipes a ringed knuckle across my cheekbone, lingering on the freckles that pepper them. His green eyes sear into me and I know that he sees me—truly sees me. Not the sunshine that the rest of the pantheon believes me only to be, but the deeper, darker shades of me that thrive in his gloam.

I am the last ember in the dying hearth, the flash of white lightning that cracks through the most torrential of storms, the dim light of the crescent moon under which the most scandalous of sins are committed.

And there are many, many sins I would like to commit with the Dark God who holds me flush against the hard stone of his chiseled chest.

The heat of his breath licks my skin as he leans close to my parted lips. "Are you still hungry, goddess?"

"Famished," I whisper against him.

Drayven nips at my lip and the tangy iron of a single drop of blood pools in its center. "May I taste you?"

The depths of his familial magic, the gift from the Goddess of Blood to her only son, have long remained a rumor amongst the pantheon. Drayca inherited a thirst for it, driving her to push mortals into more and more battles in her name.

But Drayven's inheritance is a mystery. It's said that once he has your blood, he can control you, manipulating your thoughts, actions, and feelings without your consent.

"What will that do to me?" I ask.

"One taste of your blood and I will forever be able to find you, across any realm, any time. It will bond you to me. You will be the beacon in my endless night."

Something akin to hope laces his words and colors our shared breath. A millennia of being drawn to him has culminated in this seemingly simple request. The slightest of movements and his tongue will lap up the essence of my life force, strong and full of power.

Though he doesn't say it, I can hear it all the same. One drop of my blood in exchange for the eternal protection of the Dark God of Death.

It's a small price to pay to be his to guard, his to watch—to be simply *his*. Though I don't know why, a part of me longs to grant him this request.

I suck my bottom lip into my mouth, licking away the crimson drop as my eyes dance with devious delight.

"If you want to taste me," I taunt, "you will need to ask with more than your words."

"I should have known you'd want to play." His cool chuckle rumbles through me as his shadows rise up to whisk us away again. "I hope you're ready, my light."

There is an eerie calmness in the Eternal Meadows—the place where docile souls spend their eternities. A misty fog covers their paradise, making everything gray and gloomy.

I walk the stone pathway that cuts through the rolling meadows, pass by the wooden homes whose curtains blow in the phantom breeze, and trail my fingers across the ashen-colored grass.

"Go ahead, Selene." Drayven slides his hands into his pockets and leans back against the rock formation where we stand looking over the expanse of the meadow. "Do anything you want."

The right lapel of his shirt falls open, further revealing the scrawling lines of magical ink that cover his skin. I step toward him, drawn to the ever changing art that decorates the broad expanse of him. Leaning in, I let my nose drag across the tattoos that creep up his neck until they kiss the underside of his strong jaw.

"Anything?" I breathe against him.

The Dark God stiffens, a primal growl rumbling in his throat as I step back and raise my palms to the sky.

What I intend to do here will require more magic than I've wielded before. I let it pool in my waiting hands, rushing through my veins like a bursting dam.

"If you're going to stop me, do it now," I yell over the swelling surge of power.

"I wouldn't dream of it." Desire drips from his every word as I unleash the might of my power.

The ground quakes under our feet, the gray giving way to the barest hint of red as I summon more of my light. I pull deeply from the well of immortal power within me, drawing up more and more with each shaky breath. The muscles of my arms strain as I physically shape the raw light into an orb, twisting and molding it between my hands. Every ripple in its surface is imbued with my power.

My familial magic seeps out around the edges, washing over the barren meadows and leaving trails of flowers in its wake. Blooms in red, black, white, and purple cluster in the fields, with thick hedges and evergreen trees scattered throughout.

The ball of light that hovers between us grows larger as its heat begins to overtake me. A glistening trail of sweat drips down my chest, running between my breasts—a path that Drayven's shadows follow expeditiously, both cooling and igniting me at the same time.

Air ignites like fire in my lungs as I burn through my power, the glowing red light expanding with each exhalation. My vision clouds, wholly consumed by the scarlet light of the newborn sun. The tips of my feet scrape against the ground as I levitate, following the sphere's ascent into the Under Realm's sky.

Every inch of me sizzles as I drown in the fiery waters of infernal power. The entire realm trembles under the weight of my light.

Not the darkness.

Not the infinite void of Death.

My light.

Shouts ring up from the homes below—souls emerging from their comfortable shadows to catch a glimpse of the celestial body and the goddess that birthed it.

Cool bands of wispy black magic skate across my skin, wrapping around my wrists and pulling me back toward the still quaking ground. Drayven shields me from the rocks that crumble around us, gripping me by the ass and wrapping my legs around his waist. An anchor in the depthless sea of power that threatens to sweep me away completely.

"Do you still feel hungry?"

"Yes," I pant. "Feed me, Dark One."

Tattoos slither from the Dark God's skin and slip in the space between us, sliding under the silk fabric and up my slick thighs. But unlike the last time, they don't graze or tease.

My head throws back with a moaning scream as bands of Drayven's magic thrust into me. They curl and twist, stretching and filling every inch of me as the sun continues to expand. The combination of searing power and his icy magic hurtles me toward the edge of pleasure, but just before I crest, they disappear.

I groan loudly at the absence as my eyes snap back to his. "Drayven," I plead breathlessly.

The Dark God of Death captures my mouth, his tongue slipping between my lips to tangle with mine. He grips my hair, pulling my head back to make his declaration. "I've already told you, Light. You won't find release on my shadows, or my hands, or my tongue, but I plan to use them all on you anyway."

"You're a wicked god."

"Yes, but I am your god."

My chest heaves as Drayven's shadows rip open the bodice of my dress. He wastes no time taking my nipple in his mouth while he twists the other between his finger and thumb.

The red sun hangs high in the sky now, casting a scarlet glow over his white hair. I rake my fingers through it, guiding his head as he sucks. His sharp canines scrape against the tender flesh of my breast, my back arching when I feel them break the skin. But Drayven doesn't taste my blood. Instead he moves to the other, letting the crimson liquid drip down my glowing skin.

My body quivers when his fingers slide into me and my power surges again. The red sun vibrates as our sweat mixes with my blood. Drayven holds perfectly still. I roll my hips, chasing the pleasure he denies me as the glowing star stretches overhead.

"Do you like it here?" he growls, more animal than man, as I ride his fingers.

"Yes," I breathe.

"Good." He licks the column of my throat, tasting the magic that coats my skin. "Because it likes you. It wants to bow to you."

A column of shadows forms in my peripheral, morphing into something. He spins me with preternatural speed, depositing my ass gently on the now-materialized velvet seat. Scrawling black ink twines with the taut veins of his forearms as he leans in, clutching the arms of the chair and towering over me.

"And now it will," he declares. "I have given you a realm to shape and a throne from which to rule it. May I taste you now?"

I take in the gilded chair the king crafted for me. It's smaller than his, but outshines it in both material and splendor. Each spire rising from the back of the throne is sharpened into an immaculate point, their heights varying like the rays of a sunburst.

Perfect for the Goddess of Light.

Power vibrates in my veins, tempting me to complete the metamorphosis happening in the sky, but I don't divert my attention from the deity currently licking his lips.

"Not yet," I say to both the god and the sky.

Something dark and dangerous flares to life in his emerald irises. Drayven wipes the dribble of my blood from his chin with his thumb, the silver ring glowing red under my light.

In one swift move, The Dark God of Death drops to his knees before me, rips off what remains of my gown, and tosses it carelessly to the side. "And what if I bow to you? Will you allow it now, goddess?"

The smile that blooms across my face is all the answer he needs. With the snap of his fingers, his black shirt disappears, exposing more of his inked skin. Drayven's hands grip my hips, pulling me toward him until my legs drape over his shoulders. The tattoos transform into ropes that sprout from his skin and wrap around my thighs, forcing me to open up for him.

"Look at you…naked, dripping with sweat and blood, glowing with power, and all spread out for me." Death's tongue swipes sinfully through me, his blazing eyes never leaving mine as he feasts.

Closer and closer he beckons me to the edge all while the sky screams at me, louder and louder until I can no longer ignore it. Pleasure swells within me as the single orb above separates, forming two illuminating red suns over the Eternal Meadows. As my power explodes, my muscles tighten around his tongue, euphoric release finally within reach.

I'm mere seconds away when the bastard stops.

I groan loudly as the god sits back on his heels. But the sight of me glistening across his chin and dripping down the front of his throat only intensifies my need for him.

"Are you finished?" I scoff, displeasure thick in my voice.

"Finshed?" He laughs rakishly. "I haven't even started."

He lunges for me again but I stop him. "Enough! Fuck me, Drayven."

"You seem very comfortable ordering me around."

"I am not ordering." I swallow back the resistance that rises in my throat. "I'm asking. I'm...begging."

Drayven stands in a flash, pulling me from the throne. "A god doesn't beg, Light. And a god-queen sure as fuck doesn't ask."

He snaps his fingers and his shadows transport us again. The red glow of the Eternal Meadows gives way to the dark interior of the King of the Under Realm's bedroom. Every corner of the room drips with sensual luxury—from the dark mahogany furniture to the satin sheets and the green velvet settee.

Drayven grips my chin and forces my golden eyes to his. There's a desperation written across them that I know mirrors my own.

"Do you understand what I have given you and what I ask of you in return?"

"I do."

The vow leaves my lips without a thought. For better or worse, I trade my eternal solitude for the protection of Death himself. Protection I do not need, but want with every fiber of my being. Because now that I've tasted the abyss, I never wish to surface again.

"In all my eons of life, I have never once knelt before a god. I have never allowed another into my realm and I damn sure have never given them a throne. I worship you alone, Selene. I need to know that you know that."

"I do."

"Good." His thumb pulls down the center of my lip as his eyes rove hungrily over my naked body. "I need you to remember that, because it's going to look like I don't."

Drayven's lip crash into mine. We are a tangle of tongues and teeth, each of us drinking in the other as if we've been deprived for lifetimes.

And maybe we have.

Our powers are the antithesis of each other, but the longer I spend in his realm, the more I know they are truly the divine balance. And instead of resting on opposite sides of the scales, perhaps we belong in the middle, together.

My hands work the laces of his leather pants with deft urgency. Need coils low in my belly as I free him from his fabric cage, a moan rumbling in his chest as I stroke him.

"Get on your knees," he commands. "I bowed at your altar, now it's time for you to kneel at mine."

Without protest, I drop to the ground, pulling his pants down as I go. My eyes flare with delight as I take in just how impressive the Dark God is. All these years of wondering are nothing compared to seeing him like this.

Drayven wraps my blonde hair around his fist and thrusts into my mouth impatiently. I look up at him from under my lashes as I swallow him down.

The mortal statues have it wrong. The Dark God of Death is honed from marble, but to cloak his magnificent body is a sin that should be punishable by eternal damnation. If they could truly see him—the deep lines and carved muscles of his abdomen and chest, the scrawling, shifting ink that dances across his ethereal skin, the verdant eyes that glow with desire—they would freely hand over their souls for the simple chance to look upon him forever.

Drayven moves harder and faster until water leaks from my eyes and streams down my cheeks. Death is not a gentle lover, but he coos words of praise all the same as he swipes away my tears.

"You take me so well." His shadows wrap around me, stroking my clit in reward as he thrusts impossibly deeper. "Your mouth was made for me."

My throat tenses around him as my own release builds again. Drayven's grip tightens in my hair and he pulls my head back roughly. He yanks me to my feet, using his immortal strength to toss me across the room and onto the large bed.

In a blurred motion, the god is in front of me again, knees pressing into the black silk bedding as he flips me onto my stomach in one fluid motion. Shadows wrap around my neck and haul me up until my back is pressed against his chest.

I catch sight of myself in the large mirror hanging on the bone wall. My body is slick, coated in sweat and desire and streaked with blood. The black wispy bands of his magic are a sharp contrast to my warm-toned skin. Drayven's green eyes lock with mine in the reflection.

Slowly, he drags his large hand down the smooth plane of my stomach, descending to the swollen, sensitive area he's been teasing all day. A whimper escapes from my throat when his fingers brush across it.

"Eyes on me, my light," he commands as he positions himself at my entrance. "I want you to watch the first time you take me."

Drayven pushes into me, inch by sinful inch. My eyes roll back on a moan and he stills.

"Ah, ah, ah," the Dark God tsks. "If you want all of me, you will open your gorgeous fucking eyes and watch."

He growls in delight when I meet his gaze again in the mirror, rewarding me with another inch. Drayven moves agonizingly slow. I don't need time to stretch or adapt to him—his magic has already prepared me enough. I want to move, to force him to end this torture by my means, but I don't dare tear my eyes from his. He has made it clear that he's in control, and I will only be satisfied on his terms.

A shudder wracks my body as he finally pushes all the way inside me. Magic skates across my skin as Drayven's mouth moves to my neck, sucking gently as his shadows hold me in place. Our sweat-soaked bodies move in tandem, the sound of our moans in perfect harmony. My power blends with his, gold and black mixing in the air around us as he ruts into me.

"Fuck, Selene," he moans as his hands knead my breasts.

"Bite me," I command.

Drayven throws his head back on a groan, his teeth glinting in the golden light that surrounds us. His tongue grazes across the sharp points of his fangs as his eyes lock onto mine in the mirror.

"I promise I won't hurt you…" His lips brush against my neck, his hot breath pebbling my skin. "…much."

The god sinks his teeth into my unmarred skin. I gasp as they pierce me, but Drayven doesn't stop moving. His tongue laps up the blood that leaks from the wounds as he thrusts harder. Something in my chest tightens, like a rope tying around my sternum and pulling taut—forever connecting me to the King of the Under Realm.

Drayven uses his teeth to open his own wrist and offers it to me. "Drink," he orders. "Just a taste."

I pull his wrist to my mouth and let the coppery liquid coat my tongue. Heat spreads through my body as Death's blood mingles with mine. I feel his magic invade my every sense, solidifying the bond between us.

He pulls my hair, forcing my eyes back to the mirror to watch as he fucks me harder and faster. Blood runs from the corners of my mouth and from my neck, streaming across my breasts.

I am lost in him, and if I never find my way out, I will die happy with the Dark God of Death buried inside me.

Drayven's breathing turns to pants and I know he's close. He unleashes another primal growl as his hold on me tightens.

"Who is your god?"

"You are."

"Say it again."

"You are my god, Drayven."

"And you are mine, Selene. In every sense of the word. Now be a good little goddess and come on my cock."

The words have barely left his mouth before I tighten around him. Wave after wave of divine pleasure wash over me in a blinding, brilliant light. He never strays, holding the pace until I'm certain I can't possibly come again.

But like he has all day, Drayven proves me wrong.

CHAPTER 9

DEATH

A sharp, stabbing pain jerks me from the best sleep I've had in centuries. The golden goddess asleep on my chest stirs at my movement but doesn't wake. I brush a blonde curl from her cheek, lingering on the freckles that dance upon it.

This moment—with her draped across me, naked, euphoric, and completely mine—is everything I have always wanted and never dared to hope for.

Eternity in an endless void has provided me with more than enough time to contemplate my abysmal existence. I've spent years sitting on the once gray hills of the Eternal Meadows watching the souls yearn. They call out, longing for things lost to them. I used to wonder what it might be like to have something—or someone— worth that kind of eternal devotion.

But I do not wonder anymore. Selene is worth more devotion than my miserable, immortal soul will ever be able to provide her.

The pain radiates again and I know it will only get worse the more I ignore it.

Not yet. Please, not yet.

The tattoos across my chest realign, transforming to create a sunburst halo around Selene. They cradle her head, never leaping from my skin while they crown the goddess in onyx ink.

My gaze snags on a single lock of her blonde hair still tipped in red—blood that I must have missed when I bathed her. She still smells of the pomegranate soap I used to scrub away the evidence of our depravity. Every inch of her was washed and kissed clean, this queen who will hate me soon.

The pain stabs me again.

"No." I defy it even though I know it's no use.

"Dray?" Selene's sleep-heavy voice whispers against my bare chest. She turns, lifting her golden eyes to mine. "What's wrong?"

"Everything."

"What do you mean?" Her wild curls cascade over her shoulder as she sits up. "Talk to me."

Words dry up like chalk in my mouth. There's so much I want to say to her but I can't. The Under Realm won't allow me to tell her the truth, and my feelings without that context will do nothing but hurt her.

"You have to go."

"What?" she asks. "Why would I go?"

"We had a bargain, Selene. One day in the Under Realm. That is all you were granted."

Her face contorts with confusion as she tries to sort through my carefully guarded words. "Then grant me more. If this is about the bargain, I'll make another one."

"It doesn't work like that."

"Then tell me how it works," she demands. "You made me your queen. Surely that means something to you."

"That means everything to me, my light."

"Don't." Selene shakes her head, sliding away from my touch. "Don't call me that. If I meant anything to you, you wouldn't do this. You don't want me to stay."

"That's not true." I try and fail to find a way around the rules

I'm bound to uphold. "I could give you a million reasons why I want you to stay, but there will always be one reason that you cannot. And even I don't have the power to change that."

"Are you not the king?" she scoffs boldly. "Is this not your realm?"

"No," I whisper, a single tear beginning to form in the corner of my eternally emotionless eyes. "I mean, yes, I am the king, but only in name."

I let every emotion, every confession, fill my eyes as I grip her by the face and force her to look at me. With every fiber of my immortal being, I will her to understand what I cannot say. The Under Realm is a prison, and while I may be its warden, I am trapped all the same. We may have made a deal, but I made my own with this realm centuries ago.

"You are alive, Selene. Only the dead can reside here."

"You reside here, Drayven. You are not dead."

Look at me. I silently scream at her. *See me, my light.*

"Is this about Taura's vision?" she asks, still not understanding.

"No, it's not about some fucking vision." My fists ball in the silk sheets as she scoots away from me again. "I granted you one day so that you'd never ask about that again."

"One day to what? To fuck me and drink my blood and play out some depraved fantasy before sending me home? Was this just a game to you?"

"I let you reshape this realm. I made you a throne and I bowed at your feet. I gave you my Creation-damned blood in return. Does that sound like a game to you?"

The confusion in her expression gives way to hurt, but it's when that pain turns to anger that I know I've truly lost her.

"It sounds exactly like something a dark and wicked god would do for sport."

"You want to talk about a wicked god, Selene? Then let's talk about the one you are set on following into war."

Tears streak down her starlit cheeks as her breath turns ragged. Fury builds with her every inhalation as she exits the bed. "You cannot play both sides in this. If you send me away, I will go to war."

I bite my tongue until blood pools in my mouth. There is nothing I wouldn't give to be able to tell her the truth. To stay here, she must give up her life. She will be forever held captive to the bounds of the Under Realm, never able to leave and never able to fulfill Taura's vision.

Without Selene, the rebellion ends before it truly begins and the prince dies.

I wave my hand and a shimmering gold gown appears on the bed. The goddess dresses in a huff, her rage multiplying by the minute.

It was selfish to bring her here, to think I could grant myself one last desire. Did I really think I could show her my world, worship her, and then let her go? Did I think I could taste her, devour her, consume her, and not spend the rest of my dismal fucking eternity missing her?

"I told you that you would hate me." It's a miserable excuse, but it's the only one I can muster.

She wipes her eyes with the backs of her hands before moving toward the swirling shadows I've created to send her back to the god realm.

"That's the worst fucking part of all of this. I don't hate you, Drayven. But I do pity you. You can send me away, but you will never be rid of me. Every time you walk your realm or look up in your study, you will see my power and think of me."

She steps into the black mass of magic, letting it spin around her feet. "And you will look back on this moment for the rest of your life and wish you had told me the truth."

"I have told you the truth," I lie, diverting my eyes as the tear threatens to crests my lashes.

"No you haven't." She sighs as the shadows cover her fully, her words piercing through the night. "You never told me you loved me."

CHAPTER 10

DEATH

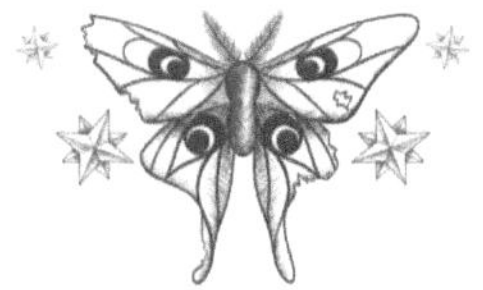

THREE MONTHS LATER

"We have already looked there, sire."

"Well then why isn't it marked off the fucking list?!" I throw the red marker at the raven that perches on the edge of the table.

"Perhaps because I do not have hands, sire?"

My fingers tangle in my hair as I grip it in frustration. "Perhaps I should remove the feathers I gave you, Corvus. Would you like to go back to being a skeleton?"

The bird hops from the table and returns a moment later with the marker in his beak. Corvus strikes 7924 from the list, crossing off the second-to-last realm before flying to my shoulder.

"You can remove my feathers, but it won't change the fact that we have searched every realm."

Fuck.

The raven is right—infuriating, but right nonetheless. I check the pocket watch for the tenth time in five minutes. The last

Reaper should have been here by now. If she doesn't have the missing god blade, months of searching will all be for nothing.

"Why do you need this blade, Your Majesty? Isn't there already one in the god realm?"

My teeth grind against one another, every muscle in my jaw flexing as I bite back my anger. "I understand that you are a bird and therefore your brain is very small, but do you honestly think Nobus would willingly hand over the only weapon capable of killing him?"

"Maybe Arcasia could smuggle it to our queen?"

I swat at the raven, shooing him from my shoulder as I turn my attention to the sky above. A month ago, the sight of these stars or mention of her would have sent me into a fit of rage, but it's desperation that takes hold of me now.

Every time I close my eyes, I see her—her face, her glowing golden eyes, the constellation of freckles across her cheekbones. And every time I open them, I see her again—her stars, her suns, the hint of shimmer that runs along the veins in my forearm now. She is impossibly interwoven into the fabric of my realm and into the very essence of who I am.

If I had known that bringing her here, that feeding her magic like that would lead to her writhing in my lap, breathless in my bed, and embedded into my heart...well, I would have done it a long time ago. What use is pretending that I would have made a different decision?

I know my sentence and I have paid my penance a million-fold. I knew I couldn't keep her, knew that the magic that chains me here and demands my silence would take her away from me, but I did it anyway.

From the moment Taura told me Selene's future, I knew this was my only chance to have her. One day with her was worth the disdain she'll harbor towards me for the rest of her existence.

And in order to have that existence, I need to find the missing god blade.

This weapon is my only chance to save her from a fate worse than mine. I nearly scoff at the irony. The weapons designed by Creation to kill their powerful children have now become the only thing that can save them.

Two identical daggers were forged in the fires of life, their handles made of ivory bone. The gods of Flesh and Blood, the first of Creation's divine children, were each gifted a blade. Gods may be injured, their flesh torn and their blood spilled, but they will not die unless a god blade is used.

The magic of Death is the only exception to that rule.

The Goddess of Blood was afraid that the children she tortured would turn on her, so my mother hid her blade. Little good it did her, though. She was the first god I slayed, and her death frightened the God of Flesh so much that he gifted his blade to his eldest son and tasked him with traversing the realms to kill me.

But Nobus has always been a selfish god—and he wasted no time burying the blade in his father's heart and stealing his throne instead.

With the ability to kill any god I choose, I've had no desire to find the missing dagger. Not until now. My condition of eternal servitude to the Under Realm deems that I cannot interfere in this rebellion. If Selene has any chance of slaying Nobus or saving the child god, she has to have my mother's blade.

Thunder claps behind me and I turn to face the Reaper now standing in my study. "Tell me you fucking have it."

"I fucking have it," the black-clad warrior says, pride tugging up the corners of her full lips as she pulls a bundle from her pack.

Obsidian fabric covers the steel, but the sight of the exposed ivory handle sets my heart racing.

"Well done, Amaya." I nod to the Reaper as I take it from her hands. "Where did you find it?"

"It was in some warlord's trove. I nearly got godsdamned crushed trying to retrieve it. Have you been to 1407, Your Majesty? They have insanely fast horseless carriages and flying death bugs."

"Bullets," Corvus corrects. "They're called bullets. The king finds the quality of mortals in 1407 especially interesting."

"Their penchant for evil is truly unmatched and I do love a people who grant me endless offerings."

My eyes are glued to the shining steel of the god blade as I unwrap it. Eons of age and a few millennia in a hellscape realm haven't dulled it a single bit.

It's here. It's really fucking here.

After months of searching every realm in existence, the one and only weapon that can give Selene a fighting chance is finally in my grasp.

"Amaya," I say without tearing my eyes from the blade. "You've earned your rest. Go fetch Osrus. I need him to deliver this for me."

The Reaper nods and exits my study without a word. Corvus soars to my shoulder, incessantly tapping his talons in an effort to get my attention.

"What?" I finally ask.

"You don't have to send Osrus. Your time is up, Your Majesty."

The raven is the only being who knows the extent of my sentence to the Under Realm, the only creature who can speak the words I am forbidden from saying.

Not that anyone would believe me anyway. A king, bound and gagged, forever cursed to serve a realm he supposedly rules— any sane person would laugh at the joke.

But it isn't a farce. For every one day I spend elsewhere, I am imprisoned in the Under Realm for one month. And if I was to try to circumvent that rule, I would cease to exist, crumbling into dust and blowing away in the wind. My immortality is tied to the confines of the dark void I call home. My eternal penance for being born with the power of death to a savage goddess.

"I think our queen is worth it, don't you?"

I don't waste my precious time responding to Corvus' question. It was rhetorical anyway. He's seen me these past three months—three whole fucking months since I kicked her out of my bed and shattered the fragile bond I insisted we make. I've been even more sullen and shuttered than usual.

Looking into his beady black eyes, I can tell the raven knows the lengths I would go to for Selene, maybe even more so than I do.

I shove the wrapped blade into my jacket pocket and, in a flurry of darkness, I reopen the blood connection between us and call to the shadows to lead me to my light.

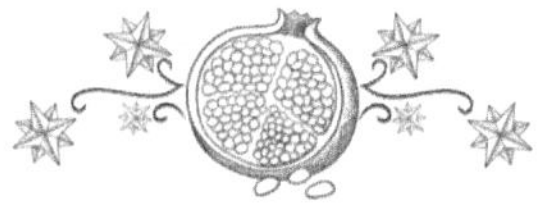

A mist covers the gardens of Nobus' palace, tinged purple by the light of the two suns that shine beyond the mountains. Of all the thousands of the realms in existence, I should have known she'd be here.

Her blood pulls me toward her, like an invisible rope tied around my sternum. I follow it through the hedges and down the river stone paths as if my very life depends on reaching her.

And maybe it does.

"Have you come for me at last, Dark God?"

The voice startles me, my feet stopping so fast that my immortal grace is the only thing that prevents me from falling over. I turn toward the voice, to the goddess sitting on the stone bench holding a sleeping child.

"No," I reply. "I am not here for you, Arcasia."

"For Calaedon, then? Has his father finally decided to do it?"

The Goddess of Protection's face is hard, no hint of sorrow or worry, only resignation gracing her features. In her mind, it's a matter of time before Nobus takes the life of her son. She doesn't know that the soul of the young Prince of the Gods isn't on my list.

The toddler stirs in his mother's arms. Arcasia drops her gaze, brushing tendrils of onyx hair from his face. Silver eyes pop open at her touch and I watch her mask slip slightly. If I was here for the boy, she would beg me to take her too.

The place where my cold, shriveled heart should be aches.

This child is so small, yet already so powerful. He's not just covered in magic, but also in love. The love of a mother who would give up eternal life to never be separated from him, and the love of gods who joined a rebellion at the sight of his eyes alone.

I saw it that night, the ripple of realization across the faces of the gods who hadn't yet agreed to join Mikais' rebellion. Across the face of the goddess I'm actually here to see. An entire section of the pantheon plots against the man who would kill this prince simply for the crime of being born.

It's a crime and a punishment I know all too well.

The image of the Goddess of Blood flashes in my mind's eye.

War clings to her leg, standing amongst her flowing skirts while my mother holds the lifeless carcass of a raven in her hands.

"That was my offering, you careless child! How dare you steal from me!"

She drops the bird and strikes me again across the face, my blood joining the bird's on her fingers.

"Every drop of blood spilled is mine. *The power of life and death belongs to me. ME! Not you. Never you."*

"Your Majesty, it's time to go now." The voice of a servant rips me from my memory. "Your allotted time is up."

Arcasia clears her throat as she rises, her gray eyes locking onto mine in a final, desperate plea to take them both. I can't tell her what I know—that the child won't die but will grow up under someone else's care, that the Goddess of Light will steal him away with the dawn—but I can grant her one sliver of hope for now.

"Not today, goddess."

She nods in thanks as the servant leads her back into her gilded prison, her head held high as the invisible noose around her neck tightens slightly.

The servant will tell Nobus what she saw and the king will summon me. I need to get to Selene before word of my presence reaches him.

The rope tied to my body tugs again. I let my shadows conceal me as I move—a quick walk that increases speed rapidly. The stronger the blood bond between us becomes, the faster I move. I have never in my life ran toward someone, never felt the sharp stab of fleeting hope that grips me tighter in her vice with each passing second.

Hope.

For the first time in my life, I feel hope.

There's a possibility that she won't see me, that she won't open the door or let me gaze into those sparkling golden eyes. But there's a possibility that she will, and that is what I cling to now.

My feet skid to a halt outside the library and I know without a doubt that she's inside. I scan the rows of shelves and find the room empty except for the glowing light near the reading alcove.

My shadows race ahead, blazing an eager path between the stacks. Selene's muffled gasp sounds when they round the corner and give away my approach.

Midway down an aisle lined in leather-bound tomes, I stop.

The golden edges of her aura seep between the books that separate us.

"Goddess."

"What are you doing here?" Her voice is flat and powerful. No hint of hatred or the misery that plagues me.

"I am here to see you."

"You're here to *see* me? Three months and that's the best you could come up with?" Her sharp words sting like the first slice of a blade across flesh.

I reach out and remove the book that separates us, instantly meeting her gaze. It's strong and fierce, but the hint of silver in the corner of her eye gives her away.

"I have made many mistakes, Selene. And I am here to..." My voice nearly breaks as the single drop pools on her bottom lashes. "To make a pathetic fucking attempt at saving you."

"I do not need you to save me, Drayven. I showed you what I am capable of. I am the Goddess of Light and the Queen of the Under Realm. Or does that not mean anything?"

The goddess walks out of view. I chase after her like a dog, removing book after book until we're eye-to-eye again.

"Selene, wait. You must understand."

"What? What must I understand? I gave you all of me, my power, my blood, my heart...and I thought you were doing the same. But when push came to shove, you lied."

"I didn't lie. It's...it's..." I stammer over my words, searching and failing to find anything that would make a difference in this moment other than the truth. "There are things I cannot tell you."

Selene scoffs. "How convenient."

"Selene, listen to me!" My temper slips, the floor around us rumbling slightly before I regain control. "The magic that binds me to the Under Realm has..." I painfully push through the heaviness that weighs down my tongue. "...conditions."

I know she needs more—that single word isn't enough to

convince her of my honesty, isn't enough to tell her how much sending her away maimed me. Gathering the full might of my power, I attempt to force my way through the rules that bind me.

"I ccccan't…for every dddday…" The harder I push, the tighter the magic wraps around my tongue and crushes me in its grasp. "You would…ddddie…" My mouth moves silently as searing pain rips through my body. My muscles fray and threaten to split from my bones as the words fill my mouth like ash.

"I want…you." I finally rasp out the only truth I am capable of and collapse to my knees. Sweat slicks my white hair to my brow. I claw at my clothes, ripping open the buttons of my shirt in a futile attempt to gouge out the pain in my chest.

"All I want is you. Keeping this from you…is not a choice, my light. It is a curse."

Footfalls sound on the marble floor and I am certain that she's leaving my pathetic ass to rot in a heap before the toes of golden slippers step into view.

I don't lift my head to look at her, refusing to let her see the shame and weakness evident on my face. I take the dagger from my jacket pocket, offering it to her by the ivory handle, the alloy blade still safely wrapped in its obsidian makeshift sheath.

"For you. To rid yourself of any god you choose…including me."

The blade won't truly end my life, but it will kill me all the same. It will send me back to the Under Realm immediately—and something tells me that it would hold me there for longer than any incarceration to date. Perhaps it would be long enough for the rebellion to run its course and for Selene to live out the fate that Taura saw for her. Perhaps it would be long enough for her to forget me entirely.

Selene takes the blade from my outstretched hand and squats before me. The fabric of her flowing silk gown pools around her like a golden pond. The fingers of her free hand trail through my hair—a soft, reassuring graze, the way one might console a dying animal before you end its suffering.

"Is this what you were doing all those months?" she asks. "Looking for this?"

"Yes."

Silence stretches between us but I don't tear my eyes from the floor.

"You sent me away because the magic forced you to," she finally says.

It's not a question, but a statement of fact. I don't know if I can form the words to acknowledge her. Summoning the last vestiges of strength in my body, I nod. A foreign wetness coats my cheek—something I haven't felt in over a century.

Selene adjusts her grip on the handle of the god blade. The black fabric falls away, the magical alloy glimmering in her golden glow. She leans closer and lifts my chin with the tip of the blade.

"Are you asking me to kill you, Dark One?"

I lean into it, my soft flesh leaking a single drop of blood. I force myself to look Selene in the eyes as I utter my damning confession.

"Isn't it always what we love that kills us?"

The corners of her lips tug up in a soft smile as another tear streaks down her cheek, mirroring my own.

"Are you finally admitting that you love me, Dray?"

"You have my realm, my crown, and my blood. I don't have a heart, but if I did, it would be yours. You could eradicate every shadow, illuminate every inch of caliginous obscurity, and rip the Under Realm to fucking shreds—and I would relish every gods-damned second as long as you were at my side."

The god blade clatters as it hits the marble floor. Selene's chest heaves with rapid breaths. She wants to be angry with me. I can see it in the pained tears that crest over the rims of her eyes and in the tremble of her hands—but she is just as ruined as I am.

"Are we doomed to forever be apart?"

"We can have a day or two, but…yes, Selene. Death is no companion."

She stares into my eyes, her pain morphing into determination. "Then we will take whatever moments we can get."

The Goddess of Light takes my face between her hands. Her magic skates across my skin—light and blood and something *shocking*. Disbelief courses through me as the blood bond between us pulses with the unmistakable flutter of a tiny heartbeat.

Conception within the Golden Pantheon doesn't happen at random. There are neither risks of accidental pregnancies nor the need to prevent them. Each and every god is divined by Creation, and only Creation has a say in the timing and the parentage.

"Selene." I rise my knees, my hands moving to cradle her face as I take in the gravity of her revelation.

The maker of all gods has decided that the pantheon needs a child with our combined gifts—and needs it now. I shudder at the thought.

What kind of god will be birthed from Death and Light? What powers might they possess? What horrors might they inherit from me?

"We have the chance to bring this child into a better world." Selene's face alights with blessed assurance. "The final battle in Mikais' rebellion is happening tonight."

The rebellion. *Shit.*

I stand abruptly, pulling Selene up with me. Terror grips me as the Goddess of Truth's vision replays in my mind.

"We have to go see Taura. *Now.*"

CHAPTER 11

SELENE

It's not hard to locate the Goddess of Truth. Ever since the command came down—from Mikais or Nina, I can't be sure—Taura has been exhausting her power. The final phase of the rebellion commences, and by the time the sun rises tomorrow, we will find ourselves as victors or exiles.

Drayven leads us down the marble halls of Nobus' palace swiftly. His entire body is tense, resisting the urge to sprint. Despite his urgency, he doesn't summon his shadows to transport us in his signature wispy cloud. They flit around us, swirling over his arms and skating across the barely-there swell of my belly, eager to be called upon by the master who ignores them.

Black and red carvings come into view as we round the corner. If the gaudy ornaments weren't enough to denote that the room belongs to Mikais, the Wolf God lounging against the door certainly does.

"Death!" Mikais exclaims with surprise at the sight of the Dark God. "You have finally seen the light."

Drayven glares at the god before cutting his eyes swiftly to me and back again. He most definitely has seen the light…just not the one Mikais is referring to.

"I am not here to join your war."

Mikais chuckles, pushing off the door and stepping into Drayven's space. The God of Death squares his shoulders, slightly angling himself between me and the Wolf God. It's a barely perceptible motion, a movement easily written off as simply adjusting his stance, but I notice it for what it really is.

"I have information that may change your mind." Mikais, ignoring Drayven's cues, places both hands on the Dark God's shoulders. "Come, Death. Let's talk."

Drayven opens his mouth to speak, but the Wolf God cuts him off. "That wasn't a request."

"I need to speak with Taura. Is she inside?" I ask.

Mikais turns his head and stares blankly at me for a moment, seemingly noticing my presence for the first time. I push past him, bored of waiting for an answer from the self-centered god. The closer we get to war, the less he seems to care about how anyone else but himself fares.

I shut the door behind me loudly, a sigh of relief slipping past my lips when the gods don't follow.

"Finally," Nina sighs. "Do you have it, Selene?"

The Goddess of Flame leans over the table, her arms bracketed atop a map of the palace. Her eyes burn with the promise of fire as she glares at me from across the room.

She sent me to the library hours ago to retrieve a book—an old tome with tales and sketches of Creation. No one knows how the divine legends of the supreme being's creation of the human realms will aid us in overthrowing the God King, but when the Goddess of Truth saw it in a vision, my sister ordered me to fetch it.

"Where's the book?" my sister asks again.

"I couldn't find it," I lie. The title flashes in my mind—the gold foil lettering on the worn brown leather. I had just pulled the book from the shelf when I felt Drayen's presence.

Taura cuts her eyes to me, the irises shifting hues as she narrows them. The corner of her lip tilts up in a smile confirming my suspicion. She knows exactly what I found in the library—and that's why she sent me there in the first place.

"Do I have to do everything myself?" Nina snaps, pushing off the table. "Mikais goes for a walk. You can't find a simple book. Meanwhile, I'm planning an entire fucking battle." She curses forcefully under her breath as she storms past me in a rush. "Just stay here, Light. I'll give you your orders when I return."

The door slams shut behind her.

"She'll be back in twelve minutes." The Goddess of Truth steps beside me, her shoulder brushing mine.

"I thought your power wasn't precise?" I bump her playfully on the shoulder.

She returns the nudge with a chuckle. "It's not. I just know her."

"Taura." I turn to face my oldest friend and watch her mouth pinch into a tight line at my tone. "I know I told you that I wouldn't ask about your vision, but—"

"Things have changed," she interrupts. "And you want to know how much of this I foresaw?"

I nod and she motions for me to sit. We each take one of the gray velvet wingback chairs that face the fireplace. Alabaster wolves flank the fire that roars within, their diamond eyes glimmering in the flames.

My hand drops instinctively to my lap, my finger grazing the place where Death's child secretly grows. "Start at the beginning. What did you see at the bestowing?"

Taura reaches across the space that separates us and takes my hand in hers. Emotions war on her expression.

"It's okay. You can tell me." I squeeze her hand, urging her to continue.

"I saw you in another realm with the Prince of the Gods on your hip." Of all the things I expected Truth to say, that was not on the list. Surely she's mistaken. Surely she saw the babe in my belly instead.

"You're sure it was the prince?" I ask, skeptically.

"Black hair. Silver eyes," Taura confirms. There's no denying the child-god in question is Prince Calaedon—the mirror image of Arcasia.

My head spins trying to make sense of her truth. Why would I have the prince in a mortal realm? "Do I kidnap him?"

"I can't be sure. All I know is the prince is with you as a child. The next vision I have of him isn't until he's older." Blue shifts to violet as Taura calls upon her power to reveal more of the truth.

"It's just snippets," she laments. "On a battlefield in tears, in a dungeon covered in blood, and...and...in Nobus' throne room crowned in shadows." The goddess' eyes return to normal, the hint of fear still lingering on her features.

She wouldn't have told Drayven that I was with the Prince without a valid reason. The rest of her vision—the prince as a man with Death's magic— that's public knowledge. Drayven wouldn't make a bargain to keep me from knowing what he openly declared in front of the entire pantheon. He wouldn't have handed over his realm for that. There must be something else I'm missing— some reason that he cares about what happens next.

"What else did you tell Death, Taura?"

"Selene." She shakes her head in dismissal, turning my confusion into intrigue.

"I know it's about me. Don't I deserve to know?"

"Of course you do." The Goddess of Truth shakes her head again as she reluctantly presses on. "I saw you in the mortal realm. You were..."

"With the prince," I finish when she doesn't. "You already said that."

"Dying," she corrects. "You were dying, Selene. He was there to collect you."

I scoff in disbelief. We are immortal. We do not die.

But that's not true, is it? Why else would I have burned my father's body on a funeral pyre in a mortal realm? His death was his choice, but ours won't be. If we're purposefully cut off from this realm, if we're exiled with no way to ever return here, we will all die.

"Did you see any of the others?"

"I am not certain of the outcome," Taura says, reading the question I artfully avoid asking. "There's still something undecided."

"Taura, I need to ask you for a favor but you cannot tell anyone. Especially not my sisters or Mikais."

The Goddess of Truth nods. I squeeze her hand tightly and guide it to rest atop my stomach. "I need you to read a fate."

Her jaw drops at my request. "Are you ..." The question dies on her tongue as her indigo eyes shift, transitioning from blue to purple as she uncovers my secret. The violet hue disappears and my best friend drops to the ground in front me.

"Holy Creation." Her expression flits from panic to awe to excitement in rapid succession. "There was so much I couldn't see before. But this...this changes everything about the prince's story. She changes everything."

"She?" I ask, tears clouding my vision.

Taura gasps as her pupils dilate again. "She has emerald eyes. Her father..."

Water streams down my face as I nod in confirmation. The goddess jumps to her feet, and begins pacing in front of the fireplace. Her hands ball into fists and flex repeatedly as she pieces together the fate of the Prince of the Gods and the daughter of Death.

"She's with him," Taura finally says. "In the throne room. They're covered in blood and wearing crowns made of shadows. She calls him Callan and he calls her…he calls her…*holy fucking Creation.*"

It's a rare occurrence for the Goddess of Truth to be rendered speechless, and whatever she's seen has now done that twice in the nearly twelve minutes since my sister left.

Taura's violet irises fade into pools of pitch black as a prophecy tumbles from her red lips. "The one with the power to unite them will rise."

"We don't dethrone Nobus, they do." The words have barely left my lips when the door to Mikais' chamber opens.

Taura quickly turns to face the fire, putting her back to the trio of deities who enter. The Wolf God, the Goddess of Flame, and the Dark God of Death stride into the room, each wearing a different expression.

Nina's face is hard and determined. The face of a commander preparing for battle.

Mikais wears a grin, a cocky expression fit for a man who believes he'll be king soon.

Drayven's face is blank, but his eyes give him away. He's anxious to hear what I know.

The thud of a book on the table pulls my attention from him. "You left a mess in the library, but I found what you couldn't."

"Sorry, Nina. I'm…nervous," I lie. It couldn't be further from the truth, though. Armed with the knowledge that only Taura and I share, I know exactly what I must do.

"Nothing to be nervous about, Light." Mikais perches on the table, crossing his ankles with a casual ease that only he feels. "We'll use our powers, maim a few immortals, and this time tomorrow my brother will be…what's the word you used, Death? Contained?"

"Not by you." Taura turns to face the Wolf God.

"Doesn't matter who does it. It just matters that it happens," he replies. "Does it happen, Goddess of Truth? Will Nobus be contained."

A smile blooms across her face, her eyes flitting to me briefly before responding. "He will be."

CHAPTER 12

SELENE

Sweat coats my palms as I pace the corridor outside of the queen's chambers. This might very well be the biggest risk I've ever taken. I may be a lot of things, but I could never be cruel enough to steal a mother's child. Convincing Arcasia to give him up on her own is the most painless way to save them both.

The door cracks open and a servant dressed in a flowing white robe motions for me to enter. I slip the sack of gold coins into her apron pocket as I step past her.

"I can only give you a few minutes. Make them count." The woman closes the door behind as she leaves, the thud echoing through the grand foyer of Arcasia's rooms.

There's a coldness here, embedded deep into the tapestries, rugs, and furniture. The kind of cold that seeps through your clothing and buries itself in the marrow of your bones. A shiver snakes down my spine as I begin my search for the goddess.

Her drawing room, her bedroom, her bathing chamber—they're all empty, pristine, and untouched. Chambers that might as well belong to a ghost.

The moment her pregnancy became public knowledge, Nobus

confined her here. *For protection*, he claimed. As if the Goddess of Protection needed anyone, no matter how powerful, to keep her safe.

No, her sentence here is about control. Why else confine a queen for two years other than to break her?

A humming sound draws me further into her tomb-like quarters. The soft, melodic noise, both soothing and haunting, stops when I step into the nursery.

Arcasia sits beside the window, the dying light from the evening sun streaming across her face, illuminating the raven hair that cascades down her body in waves.

"Have you come for him?" she asks, her eyes never leaving the sleeping toddler cradled tightly in her arms.

"No."

"Light?" she asks in disbelief as her eyes meet mine. "Of all the gods I thought would come to kill my son, I never once thought it would be you."

"I am not here to kill anyone, Arcasia. I'm here..." I open and close my mouth several times, the weight of my gamble nearly too much to bear. "I'm here to...bargain with you."

A dry, broken laugh cracks in her throat. "A bargain? Selene, I am a prisoner here. I have been stripped and deprived of offerings for so long that I barely have enough power left to protect my son. What could I possibly have that you want besides his life?"

"I want him to live," I reassure her. "I want to save your son from his father, but in order to do that, I need your word that you will keep the information I am going to give you a secret."

"If I aid the rebellion, he will kill us both," she says matter-of-factly. "Do not expect me to play games of thrones and kings when my child's life is at stake."

As long as Arcasia believes that I'm here on behalf of the rebellion, she will never believe me. My hands move to rest across my belly as I prepare to offer her the only thing that will convince her of my true motives.

"My child's life is at stake, too."

The goddess tilts her head, her eyes roving over my body. "Your child?" she asks, skeptically.

"Mikais didn't send me." I take a steadying inhale before pressing on. "In fact, this could likely jeopardize the entire rebellion. But I need you to hear me out. From one mother to another."

Arcasia rises from the chair and deposits the still sleeping prince in his golden crib. She swipes a finger across his brow, brushing the strands of black hair out of his face.

"There is nothing I won't do to keep him safe," she declares. "You have never been an adversary, Light, but if I choose to trust you now and you cross me, I will make you regret the day Creation formed you."

"I would expect nothing less."

The Goddess of Protection presses a single kiss to the prince's forehead and stands to her full height. Her gray eyes pin me to the spot as she approaches, crossing her porcelain arms over her chest.

"Let's hear it then. How exactly do you propose we save our children?"

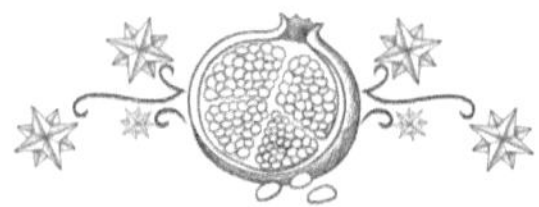

The Goddess of Song stands atop the makeshift podium, sapphire leather clinging to her curves. Lyra beams, the first notes of her song already drifting from the harp as the rebellion leaders ascend to stand beside her. Nina has donned similar armor, hers in a deep shade of ruby red.

"My brothers and sisters!" Mikais says above the crowd of gods gathered at the edge of the forest.

Creatures of all shapes and sizes linger in the treeline that marks the start of the Great Wildes—the true dominion of the Wolf God. Their eyes glow in the light from our torches as they await a command from their god.

The edges of his silver fur cloak whip in the wind as he raises his voice. "Welcome to the beginning of the rest of your lives."

Cheers ring up from the crowd, the animals roaring and chittering in agreement. Nina's flaming torch casts a sinister shadow across Mikais' face as a smile forms on his lips.

"For too long we have suffered under my brother's rule. For too long we have bent to his will. We deserve to live how and where we want. We deserve to feel the full might of our power again. No more offerings to him. No more kneeling at the feet of a god who loathes us. Tonight, we take back our realm and we take back our lives."

Something dangerous ripples throughout the crowd as the cheering resounds again. Hope, deadly and blinding, fuels the fire ignited by the Wolf God's call-to-arms. I search the faces of the gods around me and find it splayed across each of them. I commit their faces to memory, knowing that this may be the last time we all stand together in this realm.

Taura squeezes my hand gently as she does the same. She has read the fates of too many of us to still believe that we win this rebellion. It's true that fate can be changed, but the only way this outcome changes is if we do not fight at all.

The energy buzzing from the deities that gather here is not one of submission. The fire has been lit and now we will all burn.

A pair of green eyes glow in the distance. I slip back into the shadows toward their owner as Nina begins to read off the plan of attack and the role each god will play in the battle ahead.

"Last chance to run away," Drayven says as I approach. "You could hide out in another realm until this is over."

"You know as well I do that this is a long way from over," I reply. "And the prince doesn't live without me."

"So it's decided then? She agreed?"

I slip the two daggers from the sheathes hidden in the sides of my black leather pants. "You could say that."

Drayven's eyes go wide at the sight of both god blades. The blade he found and the one Arcasia stole from her husband, reunited at last after millennias apart. He takes one from my hand, turning it over.

"Is this…" His words trail off as he examines the new addition to the weapon. Arcasia's markings, sigils of her protection, run down the center of the alloy blade.

Death pricks his finger with the point of the god blade. A single drop of his blood lands atop the symbols, each glowing a brilliant shade of cerulean as the divine liquid runs across them.

"She imbued them with her magic." Drayven's awe shifts to wicked delight. "How did she know they can be altered if they're brought together?"

"Turns out that book wasn't completely useless."

"Clearly. When he notices this is missing…" Drayven pushes his white hair behind his ear as his voice trails off. He doesn't have to finish the sentence. We already know that Nobus will harm Arcasia for this and she knows it too.

I sheathe the blades at my sides, silently hoping the need to use them doesn't arise. The shadows grow thick around us as the Dark God pulls me against his chest and wraps me in his reassuring strength. His nose buries in my hair, breathing me in deeply.

Rising up on my toes, I twist and pull Drayven's mouth to mine. Our kiss is slow and consuming. I commit every movement to memory—from the way he tugs on my bottom lip to the way our tongues tangle effortlessly. There is no part of him I don't want to remember.

Any moment now, Lyra's battle cry will sound. We both know I am about to march into an unwinnable battle. A lost cause. But instead of feeling scared, I am determined.

I am not a cog in the wheel, I am the linchpin. The future of the Golden Pantheon rests on my shoulders and in my womb. I am the Goddess of Light and the Queen of the Under Realm.

And I have a plan to save us all.

Drayven breaks the kiss first. The backs of his knuckles trail across my cheekbones as he stares into my eyes. I grant myself the briefest indulgence, a fleeting second spent drowning in the infinite depths of his gaze.

In this moment, I understand why simpering mortals fall to their knees and beg for our favor. Gods do not pray—there is no higher power who watches over us. There is no one to hear our pleas, no being who grants us the desires of our hearts. There is no one to save us but ourselves.

"Meet me at the overlook just before sunrise."

Drayven presses his forehead against mine, our lips grazing one final time. "I will always meet you, my light."

The deep bass notes of a harp pierce the shadows and I know it's time. I steal one last look at the god who stole my heart before I step out of the shadows.

Lyra's song echoes through the Great Wildes, her magic spearing the souls of the waiting deities, commanding their powers to rise up and meet her. The Goddess of Song throws her head back with one final roaring note and the end begins.

CHAPTER 13

DEATH

The wild, heedless song of magic washes through the God King's palace. It calls to me, urging me to join in the battle. Blood coats the floors, veins of crimson spidering across the white and gold marble. Flames climb the curtains and engulf the oil paintings that decorate the walls. Glass shatters as a god is thrown casually through the floor-length window.

It's complete and utter mayhem—and I fucking love it.

The gods cannot die, but that doesn't stop them from beating the living shit out of each other. Grunts and screams resound from every room.

I hover like the omen I am, lingering to watch the deities bleed. My sharp canines itch to descend, to morph into the creature that roams wild in the Under Realm. To taste their blood and devour their immortal souls.

The air smells of carnage. I gulp it down greedily as I step over their writhing, mangled bodies. Bloody bootprints mark my path through the once-pristine corridors.

Room after room is the same—more bloodshed, more injured gods—but no Nobus. The Golden Parthenon is doing its best to annihilate each other while their king, the supposed catalyst for this rebellion, is nowhere to be found.

A breeze floats in through a broken window, carrying her smell. I tug on the bond and find Selene still in the palace, and more importantly, uninjured. I follow it, allowing the obsidian bands of my dark magic to search ahead of me.

A burst of light cuts through my darkness as Selene battles a trio of gods who are no match for her power, even combined. One by one, she thwarts their advances, granting no mercy and sparing no injury. Their blood hits the floor, their unconscious bodies quickly following.

A satisfied hum leaves my throat at the sight of my queen. Magnificent, powerful, and all fucking *mine*.

I am lost in her, adrift in the golden sunbursts of her eyes, wholly ablaze in her light. I take a step toward her, a depraved desire taking root in me. Every part of me wants to devour her, to strip her bare and consume her in their pools of her enemies' blood.

Selene's chest heaves with labored breaths. Even now, my darkness sings to her, a siren's song tempting her to give into the shadows that hover at the edges of her light. She swallows thickly, stepping away from my advance.

"Sunrise, Drayven. Don't be late."

The Goddess of Light turns and runs from the room, pulling me from my possessive fantasy. Her power ricochets off the corridor walls as she continues her fight.

And I must continue mine. The future of my queen and my heir must be my sole focus.

I send out the dark magic again, searching every room until it locates the God King. Moments later, with nothing more than the flick of my wrist, the door to Nobus' private chambers is reduced to a pile of splinters.

The murderous eyes of the Goddess of War meet mine across the threshold.

"Sister," I drawl. "Always a pleasure."

"I don't echo the sentiment, Death." Drayca's vicious eyes echo her curse. As if her own offerings don't hand me countless souls every single day across the realms.

"I'm not here to see you."

"I'm not letting you anywhere near my king." She raises her battle axe, preparing to strike me.

"Your king." I scoff. "One day you'll call me that."

"I would sooner waste away in the mortal lands as a powerless, forgotten god than to ever bow to you." War shakes with rage as the curse falls from her lips.

My own tip up in a smirk at the sight. It is so much fun to get her riled up like this. "That can be arranged."

"I will kill you one day," she declares through clenched teeth.

"I'd like to see you try. Truly. I can't imagine how fun it will be."

Drayca swings her axe with every intention to slice me in half. Just before her blade can graze the fabric of my shirt, I evaporate into a mass of shadows.

"I was right. That was fun," I taunt.

The Goddess of War turns to find me lounging casually on the velvet settee inside the king's quarters. Fury drips from her every pore. I breathe it in, relishing in how my delight further stokes her blinding wrath.

"That's enough." Nobus' voice booms with authority. "You're dismissed, Drayca."

"I am not leaving you with him, my King."

"War," he scolds. "I didn't ask."

Drayca's shoulders drop in resignation. A dog reprimanded by her master.

"A delight, as always, sister." I pick a sliver of wood off my shirt, casually dropping it on the floor without looking at the goddess whose ire still vibrates through the room.

"Have you come to fight for me, Death?" Nobus takes the seat across from me, crossing an ankle over his knee with a flippant ease as my sister leaves to join the battle.

"I will never give an offering to War. I am simply here to feast on the souls of dead gods."

Nobus chuckles. "You know they're not dying. Come now, tell me why you're really here, Dark God. Or should I finally see my father's request through and end your pathetic immortal existence?"

Gods, I love when my assumptions are correct.

Contrary to what the mortals believe, there are fates worse than death. And, just like I thought, Nobus plans to make the rebel gods suffer. Why end them when he can cut off the rejuvenating source of their power, end their offerings, and force them to live in pain with no hope of the sweet relief my power offers?

"I am here to make a bargain with you." It's a risky gamble to taunt the God King even in the most peaceful of times. But Nobus is a cocky god and I plan to offer him something he can't resist.

"A bargain?" Surprise flares in his eyes before he chuckles again. "If it's souls you want, I'm afraid you'll be hungry. They will not be entering the Under Realm any time soon."

"Exile." The single word piques the God King's interest as I bait the hook. "Am I right?" I know I am, but the single nod of his head confirms it. "Exile them to 717."

"What?" Nobus asks, not hiding the spark of shock that shimmers in his golden eyes.

"That's my bargain. You agree to exile the rebels to Realm 717 and, in exchange, I will tell you what the Goddess of Truth withheld from you. The real truth about the future of your realm."

Nobus straightens in his seat, every muscle in his jaw tightening in restraint. His breathing changes slightly, and I know he's taken the bait. Now it's time to set the hook.

"717 restricts their power," I explain. "The strongest will be able to wield an element, maybe two, but the rest will be without magic. And what is a worse fate for a god than to be forgotten and powerless?"

"Powerless." The word rolls languidly in his mouth as he considers my offer.

This particular mortal realm will end their suffering and kill them sooner than the others, but Nobus doesn't need to know that. The image of Gaius the Green's funeral pyre replays in my mind, the great god burning after only a handful of years of his chosen life on 717. Of course the God King doesn't remember that. He would never concern himself with remembering facts about anyone other than himself.

"Why do you care, Death?" Nobus asks, his words laced with suspicion. "What's in it for you?"

"Convenience," I lie. "It's easier to keep tabs on them if they're all confined to the same realm. No scouring the ether to clean up their messes and reap the mortal souls they'll take. And, lucky for you, you only have to seal one doorway to make sure they don't return, not thousands."

Nobus stares inquisitively, weighing my words and inspecting them for any hint of a trick. Seconds pass and I grow more impatient with every tick of the clock. He's taking entirely too fucking long.

"Think about it. If you send them all to a magicless realm, the influx of magic will give the mortals proof of your existence," I say, preparing to stroke his ego. "They'll have no choice but to worship at the feet of the all powerful God King. Think about how your power will grow with their offerings."

I swallow down the bile that arises at the revolting words. Giving Nobus any modicum of praise makes me want to be physically ill. But, right on cue, his eyebrows lift and the muscles in his jaw ticks—and I know I have him now.

"Bulk exile to Realm 717 in exchange for the truth," Nobus repeats the offer.

I nod once in agreement, willing my expression to remain blank. If he has the slightest inkling how this truly benefits me, he'll never agree to it.

Life in this particular mortal realm, the one that meant everything to her father, is the only peace I can offer Selene. That and the promise that her suffering will not last forever.

"Done," Nobus declares, extending his arm towards me. My gaze flicks to his tan hand to his golden eyes.

"The heir will reunite the pantheon." The paraphrased prophecy echoes in the room with the ferocity of a wrecking ball in a silent hall.

Those weren't Taura's words exactly, but they have the intended effect all the same.

The god retracts his still outstretched hand. "When? How?" he demands. "That's not possible."

"See that's the thing about the truth, Nobus. No one can escape it, even you."

"I cannot die!" he roars. "I made a deal with Creation. I am the exception."

I lick my lips, tasting his fear in the air around us as I provoke him further. "No one said anything about you dying, but feel free to keep speculating. It tastes delicious."

"I should kill you."

"But I'm not done, Your Majesty, " I mock. "I've seen your son in the Under Realm...on his knees."

Nobus' fists ball at his sides, perfectly playing into the chess match I've laid out before him.

The length of my presence here is precisely timed. While I occupy the God King, the Goddess of Protection smuggles their son out into the night. The Prince of the Gods may have been born a lamb destined for slaughter, but it's a man that kneels in my throne room in the Goddess of Truth's vision, not a child.

"Crowned in *shadows*." Nobus repeats the snippet of the prince's fate that has no doubt replayed in his mind since the bestowing. "No son of mine would ever bow to you, Dark God. You must trick him! Why else would he have your power?"

"I couldn't tell you," I say, leaning forward to meet the god's challenging stare. "And furthermore, I could not care less who sits their immortal ass on your cursed throne or how they get there. I do not play your games or fight your wars. I am a king and I only do what serves me and my realm. What happens to your son is of no concern to me."

The half lie tastes strangely bitter on my tongue, a sensation I am not familiar with. Once the prince is delivered to the mortal realm, once Selene's life is no longer tied with his, I won't care. I won't even spare the boy another thought.

"Prove it." Nobus calls my bluff. "Swear it in blood at the altar of Creation that you will not give your magic to the Prince of the Gods and I will uphold my end of our bargain."

Taura often says that fate can be changed if only one is strong enough. I don't know how the child gains my dark magic, but I hope for his sake that he's strong enough to overcome whatever curse I am about to deliver to him.

Terror mixes with magic in my veins as the reality of our destination settles in. My last visit to the altar was a century ago, and every part of my being hopes that Creation does not wish to summon us to their realm.

With a deep inhale, I push down my fear, drink in Nobus' desperation, and stand to my full height.

"Lead the way, God King."

CHAPTER 14

DEATH

Nobus' power vibrates through the throne room as the gods of the Golden Pantheon kneel before him. His magic grips them by the throat, wrapping around their necks like glimmering collars. Their immortal bodies, still coated in fresh blood and torn clothing, tremble under the weight.

Mikais lies unconscious on the dais. Nobus raises his foot, firmly planting it atop the barely rising chest of his brother as he further taunts the crowd.

"Did you think I could be so easily overthrown? That my brother could save you from me? What a joke."

He pushes up, straightening his leg. A crunching sound echoes in the room as Mikais' breast bone breaks under his weight. A day, maybe two, and the god will be as good as new. Damaging the Wolf God's body is simply a display of power and control.

Several gods in the crowd wince at the noise, and one even cries out in agony for the public face of the rebellion. But the true leader, the one who planned this battle and ensured a level head ruled over emotions, glares at the God King with flaming eyes. I have no doubt that the dais would be fully engulfed in Nina's fire if Nobus' magic didn't suppress it.

From the recesses, I watch, lurking in the shadows. The wound on my hand itches as it heals, the only evidence of my blood promise disappearing rapidly. I roll the sleeves of my black shirt up before shoving my hands into the pockets of my pants.

Look at ease. Don't give yourself away.

I am here as a threat, an ominous presence meant to stoke their fear. And I am that to many of them, but I am not that to her. Selene's head hangs in apparent resignation—all a part of the game still very much at play.

"This is the god you would elevate to *king*? This is the god you would sacrifice your immortal existence for?"

Nobus flicks his hand, causing Mikais' body to tumble down the stairs like a bouncing ball. The God King stomps forcefully after him, bending at the waist and gripping Mikais by the hair. Nobus lifts the limp body of the Wolf God above his head. A bloody, desecrated show of just how merciless he is, even toward his own brother.

"The price for his treason is your life in exile."

Denial fills the room as the gods take in their sentence. I can taste their fear, their surprise, their disgust. I step out of the darkness, allowing myself to be seen.

Countless eyes flit in my direction, eyes that silently beg for me to claim their souls instead. Shimmering bands of dark magic roll through the crowd, twisting and turning around the gods but remaining just out of reach.

The first notes of a song follow alongside them. Lyra's cracked voice squeaks out a haunting dirge around the magical collar that binds her. Every note is filled with a pensive sadness that settles deep in the bones of the pantheon.

The God King drops the Wolf God into a heap on the floor. He wipes his brother's blood on his white shirt, caring little for the cloth or the god who barely clings to life. Nobus climbs the dais again, planting his ass on the obnoxiously large golden throne and leaning back with casual ease. He loosens the magic that restrains the kneeling deities slightly.

"Now is when you beg," he says with a prideful smirk.

Selene glances my way, cueing my exit. She will have to beg alongside the others, and we both know I can't stomach watching it.

I make a show of drawing my magic back towards me. Shadows crack in the air like whips as they return to their wielder, a demonic smile painting my lips.

"Take me, Dark God!"

"Kill us, please!"

"DEATH!"

They scream for me as I slowly step backwards. Their pleas coat my tastebuds, my tongue salivating with their delicious distress. I want to stay, to consume it all as Nobus drags their bodies from his realm. To indulge, to savor every morsel until there is nothing left of them.

Darkness rises within me as their cries grow louder. I halt my exit, daring to sip from their emotions for a moment longer.

The hair on the back of my neck prickles as lightning flashes across the night sky. The tell-tale sign of approaching death pulls me from my feast.

The decision has been made and the goddess that awaits me on the beach now doesn't have long left on this plane of existence.

Arcasia stands in the surf, the water washing over her bare feet. The prince, strapped to her back, peers over her shoulder. From their black hair to their gray eyes, they are a mirror of each other. Two souls fated to change the future of the gods.

The child babbles something incoherent, but his mother doesn't comfort him.

"I always knew I would hand my son over to the Dark God of Death," Arcasia says. "I just never imagined it would be willingly."

"If it brings you any comfort, I won't be keeping him." I step out of the shadows and into the fading light of the two moons. "You, however, are a different story."

"So he's decided then? My husband will kill me now?"

A single dip of my head is the only response I offer her. Arcasia's fate is sealed. The goddess that stands before me now will never again walk the shores of this realm or hold her child in her arms after tonight.

"Offer me a bargain, Dark God."

Arcasia boldly steps toward me. She is frantic, yes, but there is no fear on her scent, nothing that I can drink in to temporarily satisfy the unfillable void within me.

"Who are you to demand such a thing from Death? What could you possibly offer me?" I scoff as the bands of my dark magic swirl around her in warning. Sunrise approaches, and with it, my last chance to see Selene.

"Give me the child."

Arcasia unties the fabric that holds the princeling to her back, her tears coating his cheeks as she kisses him.

My magic wraps around the him and begins to carry the prince toward me. The Goddess of Protection reaches out, her finger tracing a serpentine path on his small chest.

"*Alak ayo nora,*" she whispers in the old language. Sparkling cerulean power envelopes him at her words, a final gift from his mother.

"I know she is yours," the goddess says in a whispered breath as the child floats to my side.

"What did you say?" I demand, anger building in my veins at the implication of her words.

If she dares to threaten me, dares to try to blackmail me… whatever end Nobus has planned for her will pale in comparison to what I will do to her.

"The baby. Calaedon's fated." The goddess drops to her knees in the water, her storm cloud eyes locking onto mine. "I can still protect her. Offer me a bargain, Death."

"I cannot save you, Arcasia. I am not your judge nor am I your executioner. Beg your husband for your life."

"A favor," she calls out. "No conditions."

The shadows that swirl around my feet pause at her offer. It's true I cannot save her, but I am intrigued enough to hear her out. Her desperation may yet offer something Selene can use to save the children.

"In exchange for what?"

"My beast form," she starts. "Keep my beast form alive and I will grant you any favor. No questions, no conditions. Anything you want, it's yours."

A leviathan. A serpent. A dragon. The mortals call it various things in their realms, but each of them marvel at the beastial form of the Goddess of Protection.

I've watched her take down ships, eclipsing them with her massive scales, crushing their masts with nothing more than a casual flick of her tail. To have a creature like that under my control is tempting.

"If—and that is a very big if—if I am able to make that possible, you will never be able to shift back."

"I know."

Considering the offer, I toil over her words for any trick or deception and find nothing but hopeless anguish. If she dies and exists only as some reanimated sea beast, confined to the watery depths, she won't have access to her full power. Any magic she will need to fulfill our deal must be used now.

"You will grant my daughter your protection now and it will come to her in preparation for the moment she will need it most."

"Done." The words have barely left my lips before the blue bands of Arcasia's magic bursts forth from her body.

"I am not done." I raise my palm, halting her. "You will grant my daughter your protection *and* you will be my creature. You will do my bidding for the rest of eternity."

Pain flits across Arcasia's face as she considers my counter offer. "Eternity is a long time."

"So is death."

The goddess bows her head in resignation as her magic flares to life again. "Get me to his realm and we have a deal."

I step towards her, crouching down to grip her jaw. "How many bargains have you made tonight, goddess?"

Her eyes glow silver with a renewed fire. "None that I would not make a thousand times over to save my son."

Dark magic joins with blue as our bargain seals.

"Shift," I command. "Shift now and he will exile you with the rest of them."

"And you will keep the beast alive?"

"You question me now, goddess?" I scoff. "It's a little too late for that."

Arcasia's body shudders as my hold on her tightens. Dark magic wraps around her heart, squeezing until the goddess submits. I step back admiring the transformation.

Curls of dark hair shift into shimmering scales sharp enough to slice through muscle without thought. Her eyes grow large but keep their signature gray as she slithers backwards into the water never to surface again in this realm.

CHAPTER 15

SELENE

The wind whips my golden hair, carrying the scent of jasmine from the bushes that line the walkway to the overlook. My hands grip the marble railing as I try to steady myself from the rush of power that swells in my chest. The two suns hover below the horizon just beyond the sea. Invisible to all, but on full display for me. They sing loudly, begging to be pulled from their slumber early.

The skin on my arms prickles in the morning twilight. I take another deep breath, feeling the tug of another sort of magic swelling in my blood. He's near—and just in time.

A dark mass of shadows swirls in my peripheral before giving way to the corporeal form of the Dark God of Death. I exhale a sigh of relief, relaxing into Drayven as he wraps his arms around my shaking body.

"Do you have him?" I ask, closing my eyes and savoring the icy chill of his skin.

"I do." Drayven's nose grazes the shell of my ear, sparks alighting within me.

I turn in his hold, breathing in his scent. My hands roam over his arms, memorizing the curve of every muscle of his perfectly honed form as I prepare to say goodbye.

"What the fuck?" Nina's voice cuts through Death's intoxicating haze.

I snap my head in her direction. The Goddess of Flame's eyes burn into me as she screams in the moonlight.

"You fucking traitor!"

"Nina, no. I'm—"

"Save it, Selene." Rage burns in her every movement as she rushes towards me on the stone path. "You think you're clever, don't you? All this time you were playing me. I saw you on your knees before the God King. You begged to speak with him alone... and you begged so fucking well." Nina scoffs. "I should have known then, but I wanted to give you the benefit of the doubt. That's why I followed you from his chambers...only to find you with *him*."

"It's not—"

"What did you do with Nobus? And what the fuck is going on between you two?" She points from me to Drayven and back again.

My eyes bounce between them as I weigh my response. Which answer is the most likely to further incite her rage? Which sin can I confess first that won't make them both run away?

Nina doesn't really care what's happening with Drayven. Family doesn't mean much to gods—for Creation's sake, she didn't even attend her own father's funeral—so a betrayal from me shouldn't hurt any more or less than if it came from any other member of the rebellion.

The flames that hover at the tips of Nina's fingers are full of fury, but they spark with something far more dangerous. She still believes there's a chance to escape the fate the God King has decreed.

"Selene." Drayven grips my chin, turning my face to his. "Your sister asked you two questions and we are eager to hear your answers to both."

"I…I…" Words tangle on my tongue as I place my final bet on which to divulge first. A risk, but one I have to take. "I made a bargain with Nobus."

"You did *what*?!" Their voices are nearly in unison as both gods direct their ire at me.

"I gave him information in exchange for…" I wring my hands in anticipation of their fallout. After a shaky inhale, I breathe out the truth. "A way back home."

"I don't understand. What could you possibly give Nobus to convince him to grant that?" The Goddess of Flame steps closer. Anger still burns at the edges of her vision, the deity ready to strike if my answer doesn't please her.

"Show her," I say to Drayven. "Show her what we've done."

"Selene," he says solemnly. "Are you sure?"

"Yes." My skin tingles. I cut my eyes to Nina and see her fingers skate over her arms, too. The end of our time here has begun. "There's nothing she can do to change it now."

Drayven sighs in clear disagreement, not feeling the tell-tale sign of Nobus' impending exile. The Dark God's shadows fall away, exposing the sleeping form of the Prince of the Gods.

Nina gasps, the flames on her fingers extinguishing as she reaches out for the hovering young god.

"You kidnapped the prince?" she asks, pride overtaking her face.

"Not exactly."

Nina holds up a hand, halting me as my correction falls on deaf ears. "Holy Creation. You may have just saved us, Selene. Nobus will never exile us if—"

"He will," Drayven stops her. "He will exile all of you, alongside the prince and his mother."

My gaze snaps to the Dark God. His hand grips mine, urging me to read between the lines of his next words.

"The heir will reunite the gods."

Heir. His or Nobus', we can't be sure. And to speculate aloud would be to hand over information that I don't fully trust my sister not to use to her advantage.

It's a gut-wrenching truth, but it's true all the same. Nina's own ambitions will be the end of her one day and I cannot allow my child to be in her crosshairs.

"We didn't defeat Nobus, but he still might. That's why we have to take him with us, and why he has to have a way back home. But only the heir can use the doorway. That is what I begged Nobus for."

"What did you tell him, Selene?" Drayven asks skeptically.

"I told him..." I swallow thickly, the admission sticking like honey in my throat. "I told him that one day his son would become trapped without the ability to get home. I just didn't tell him when, where, or that I was the one taking him."

The Dark God's laugh booms through the night air, genuine amusement coloring his features.

"You crazy, beautiful fucking goddess." He plants his lips on my forehead and I blossom in the light of his praise.

"Wait...you two have been working together the entire time?" My sister backs away from the prince, confusion still etched in her brow.

"Yes," Drayven breathes against my skin. "And your sister's actions will be the reason your little rebellion succeeds one day."

"I'm sorry, Nina. I know you wanted it to be Mikais on the throne."

"Ha!" Nina's unexpected reaction startles me. "This rebellion was a power grab. Mikais was just a means to an end. The Wolf God doesn't hold a fraction of his brother's power. But if he could overthrow him, if he could dispose of Nobus for us, well...we could easily place a better ruler on the throne."

Whether the child prince that hovers in the shadows will be a better ruler is yet to be determined. But if he grows up away from Nobus' influence, he might have a fighting chance.

He could be kind. He could be merciful. He could have love in his immortal heart instead of hatred—and that in and of itself would be worth all this mess.

The ground under our feet trembles, causing Drayven to mask the child again. We lock eyes in the fleeting darkness, his emerald eyes shining in the first light of the rising suns.

"We don't have much time," I whisper.

"Flame," Drayven growls as he takes my face between his ringed hands. "Give us a moment to say goodbye."

Nina starts to reply, but before her words reach my ears, shadows encase us. Wispy bands of dark magic block us from the rest of the world as Drayven's lips crash into mine.

Time fades into nothing as the god consumes me, body and soul. There is no inch of me that he does not devour, no part of me that is not thoroughly ruined.

A stabbing sensation throbs in my chest. I ignore it, pushing past the pain to kiss him deeper. It grows sharper and more intense by the second, as if I'm being physically, methodically cleaved in two.

I pull back from Drayven slightly, staring deeply into the eyes of the deity who owns all of me.

"Don't go." His whispered plea skates across my lips, but we both know there is no stopping what is coming.

"Promise me, Drayven." The sensation intensifies, my time here rapidly diminishing. "Promise me that the next time you see me, you will take me home with you."

Home.

No matter which realm my body lives in, my heart will forever be in the Under Realm. And one day my soul will be reunited, with it, with *him*, dwelling there for all eternity.

"Promise me you will live, my light." Death's lips caress my neck, urgent kisses coating my skin as our time together further depletes. "I know you would die for me, but I need you to live for me now. Live for our daughter. Live for the future of the pantheon. Do whatever you must to ensure they succeed."

The Dark God of Death places the Prince of the Gods in my arms. The tiny life inside my womb flutters frantically, the pulse of their connection evident even now.

A flare of viridian light forces me to close my eyes and stumble backward. Drayven moves, wrapping us in his stony embrace and pulling us against his granite chest.

"She is strong." He chuckles. "But I would expect nothing less from a god of two realms."

Drayven kisses the top of my head devoutly. He slips a silver ring from his pinky onto my thumb as the earth quakes again. "Hold tight to them, my light."

"Drayven," I plead against his neck.

Darkness of a different kind clouds my vision. Not the shadows of the dark master, but the obsidian fabric of space and time. Specks of light flicker into view— individual realms, each its own world. One glows brighter than the rest and I feel my internal compass train on its coordinates.

The beautiful face of the Dark God of Death fades rapidly from view, the feel of his hold disappearing by the second.

"I love you," I call out in the darkness. "I think I have always loved you."

Drayven dissolves into bleak nothingness as I tumble through the chasm of eternity with the Prince of the Gods clutched in my arms. The connection in our blood weakens as the distance between us increases. One thin strand remains, a single string tethering me to the deity.

What remains of my body evaporates as the whispered words of the Dark God of Death fill my head. *"Alak ayo nora."*

All that I am is yours.

CHAPTER 16

SELENE

The worn cobblestone streets of the capital city are empty. Rain falls gently from the sky, water coursing through the mortar from the earlier deluge. Lanterns hanging from the doorways of homes are the only light, the moon dark and hidden from view. Constellations decorate the sky, the pale outlines of a wolf and an owl, sigils of the gods I'd sooner forget.

The scrap of worn parchment in my hand crinkles as I check it once more.

213 Regent Row, Amale

The scrawled writing matches the brass numbers that adorn the weathered door in front of me. I raise my fist and knock on the door, barely recognizing my skin. The glow of my immortal body has been traded for the pale, lifeless complexion of a mortal. The infinite power of a god diminished until I can do nothing but wield a trio of elements.

The loss of magic has been the hardest part of exile, for both myself and the tiny goddess inside me— that and the parting gift from her father. For days, I hid in the confines of an abandoned home, struggling to breathe in this realm.

The boy prince never left my side, seemingly unaffected by the change. While my body morphed and adapted to the limits of my new existence, the child clung to my side, never straying from the fate growing in my womb.

I knock again, this time with urgency as the child hidden under my brown cloak squeezes my leg tightly. The Goddess of Truth opens the door, her raven hair and violet eyes sparkling in the lantern light.

"Taura," I say in a hushed voice.

"Where is he?" she asks, motioning for us to enter.

The Prince of the Gods peeks out from underneath my cloak. He looks up at me, silver eyes locking onto my golden gaze in permission. I nod once, reassuring him of our safety here.

"Very good," the Goddess of Truth says. "Rhea, come meet your son."

A mortal woman with honey hair and a gentle smile drops to her knees slowly in front of the child, her own baby still attached to her breast.

"Hello there, little one." The soothing cadence of her voice draws the prince from hiding. "It's okay. I am a friend."

He takes tentative steps towards her, his eyes filled with curiosity. His small hands reach toward the baby in her arms, gently caressing its blonde hair.

"This is your brother. And so is he." The woman points to another child.

A boy, only a year or two older than the prince, stands in the corner. His hair is brown, a perfect match to the roughspun clothing of this country's commonfolk, but his eyes match those of his mother. Amber irises full of warmth and an innate kindness.

The child steps closer to them, carefully examining the onyx-haired boy.

"What's his name?" His small voice squeaks out.

"His true name cannot be spoken in this realm," Taura cautions quickly. "His father cannot know he is here until he's strong enough to face him."

"Callan." My hand drifts to my belly and his fated princess inside. "She called him Callan in your vision, Taura."

"Callan," Rhea repeats. "Do you like it?" She brushes the hair from his face as the prince smiles. "Yes, I think that will suit you just fine, Cal."

"Cal," the young boy says, taking the prince's hand into his. "Brother."

Rhea wraps the children in her arms as Taura takes my hand and leads me out of the door and onto the cobblestone streets. We leave the family of four, granting them the privacy to adapt to their new circumstances.

"He'll thrive here, Selene." The Goddess of Truth's irises shift from blue to purple and back again. "Tell me about the letter from your sisters."

"It seems Nina misheard everything we told her and has spread the news that *an heir will lead us back home,*" I say with a sigh. "So off they've all gone to create their own heirs."

"This land is ripe with men eager to solidify their power."

"Power." I scoff. "What do they know about power?"

"What is power if not control?" Truth falls from the goddess' lips. "They don't have magic, but they have influence and money and armies that serve them."

"My sisters will never be happy in the background serving mortal men."

"They don't need to be happy, they need to survive," she says flatly. "Look around you. Do you see luxury here?"

There is no life fit for a goddess, even a fallen one, anywhere but the palaces and manors of this realm's rulers. Patriarchy reigns supreme here and women are only worth what their bodies can provide. Marriage to these men ensures a life for my sisters twofold—a lifestyle more akin to what they're accustomed to, free from the perils of poverty, and an opportunity to fulfill a misheard prophecy.

You cannot put a price on hope, even if it's a farce.

"Where will I go?" I ask.

The princeling doesn't need me anymore. In fact, he needs none of us. The further removed from the pantheon and the influence of the gods, the better his chances of growing into a ruler worth following. Taura gave the human woman everything she'll need once his powers manifest—whenever and however that happens in this cursed realm.

Taura squeezes my shoulder. "It's not the Under Realm, but the Emerald Region might give you a sliver of comfort."

Emerald. The color of his eyes. The color of his daughter's eyes.

"You need to hurry, Light. Your lie won't hold up if you wait much longer."

Taura is the only other god in this realm who knows the truth. If I have any hope of passing this child off as a demigod—the child of a mortal man—I need to marry now.

Mikais cannot know the babe is the Princess of the Under Realm, just as he cannot know that the boy with gray eyes is the Prince of the Gods.

One day, when they're ready and destiny can wait no longer, they will find each other. The realms and mortals who raised them will never be able to suppress the cunning and ruthlessness passed down from the kings who sired them.

Mikais is just as cutthroat, but if he stands in the way of their fate, I have no doubt he'll fall.

Will I be around to see it? Do I even want to be alive that long?

I twist the silver ring on my thumb, the symbol of our love

growing heavier by the minute. My heart aches at the idea of spending what remains of my life at the side of anyone other than Drayven.

"Go," Taura urges as she slips a piece of parchment in my hands. "Go to the Eastern Sea. You'll find Arcasia in the waters and a young governor in a cottage. You need them both."

I nod in appreciation as the Goddess of Truth turns and disappears down the dark alleyway. The parchment feels heavy in my hands, and I know without reading who the missive is from.

My fingers tremble as they slip below the black wax seal, the embossed moth sigil of the Dark God fluttering to the cobblestones below.

LIVE, MY LIGHT. WHATEVER YOU MUST DO IS ALREADY FORGIVEN.

Tears fill my eyes, a single drop spreading across the letter as it falls to the parchment.

I am a goddess, but I am so much more.

This is the true measure of a woman—the ability to carry on, to swallow down her pride and discomfort and do what must be done. I don't even know the life that grows inside me, but I know I will do anything to keep her safe.

The god blades in my pocket grow heavy with promise. I could use them, these impossibly sharp blades. I could ignore Taura's words and take my fate into my own hands. I could slaughter every human in this realm one by one until I force the Reaper of Souls himself to appear and collect them—if only to see his face again, even for a fleeting second.

But that doesn't help our daughter.

I read the words again slowly, savoring every syllable, before carefully folding Drayven's letter and slipping it into the bodice of my dress against my heart. Where he will always remain until we can be together again.

The sound of laughter drifts from the open window as the princeling—*Callan*—chases his new brother playfully. I slip one of the daggers from my pocket. Black fabric covers the alloy blade and the protection runes etched into it. I make eye contact with the human woman and nod as I place the weapon of destiny on the dark wood seal.

He will need this more than I will.

With a resigned sigh, I turn and head for the Emerald Region of Corinth and the future that awaits us both there.

CHAPTER 17

DEATH

"Your Majesty." Corvus taps impatiently, his black wings puffing against my face. "Is it time?"

"Almost," I reply, shooing him from my shoulder. I adjust the lapels of my dark suit, fiddling with the fabric until I finally remove the jacket in frustration.

"Anxious?" the raven asks.

"No," I bite out, adjusting the pomegranates in the bowl for the fourth time this hour.

"Liar." Corvus plucks a single stem from the vase atop my desk, flying over to drop the dark purple bloom in my hand. "It's been a long time. It is okay to be anxious, Your Majesty."

"The Dark God of Death does not get anxious, bird."

"Maybe he does not…but Drayven does."

Corvus' beady eyes see far too much of me. But that's the way it's always been, ever since the day I killed him. He was my first death and the closest thing I've ever had to a friend.

"I'll finish the preparations; you go fetch the queen."

The sound of her name whispered in the ether pulled me from sleep in the wee hours of the morning. Ever since her name was written on the scroll of souls to be collected today, I have been preparing. From sending my Reapers to gather her favorite fruit to changing into four different black suits—all of which look and fit identical—I have been uncharacteristically nervous.

I slip the flower into my pocket and take one last look at myself in the mirror. The ink on my skin vacillates from sunbursts to crescent moons in anticipation. The overly polished rings that adorn my hands glimmer in the firelight as I smooth back an errant strand of white hair. My fingers skate over my naked pinky, the missing ring soon to be reunited with the set.

"Corvus," I say with a shaky breath. "Wish me luck."

On a deep exhale, I command the shadows to wrap around me and step into the dark void of eternity. The infinite chasm between worlds where space and time does not exist. One star stands out on the map—a fixed point in glowing viridian.

If that wasn't enough to locate her, our blood bond pulses like a honing beacon. It calls to me—*she* calls to me.

I train my internal compass on Realm 717, traveling faster than I ever have before. Moments later, my feet sink into sand.

The Eastern Sea laps against the shore, the light from the sun catching on a hint of black scales that crest in the waves. I offer a lifted finger in recognition of the creature who has come to greet me before following Selene's pull toward the cottage just over the dunes.

The weathered door opens easily, granting me entrance without knocking. Tentatively, I step into the cottage. The smell of salt and leather fills the home. Books litter the large dining table, and in a chair, slumped over the pile of tomes, sits the mortal man I have watched live alongside the goddess I love.

His sleep is light and fitful. I inch toward him to read the page where exhaustion finally took hold of him. It's a list of rare herbs, medicinal plants, and the illnesses they'll cure.

But none of them have worked on her.

What ails Selene isn't anything a human has ever experienced. Her death is a slow, painful murder at the hands of a vengeful God King. Eight years of no offerings, no worship, and severely reduced magic are what destroys her now.

Mikais wasted no time gaining power of this world and wiping all of them—every member of his rebellion—from their religious texts.

Every member except him, of course.

He erased the details of his betrayal, but left the act, and their speculation of the motive behind his treason has proven to be more than enough to sustain him.

I lay a single finger on the mortal man's temple and grant him the deep sleep he desperately needs—but mostly to ensure that he will not wake to see her departure.

Leaving him, I follow the bond to the bedroom at the back of the cottage. There, wrapped in green velvet, lies the Goddess of Light. She doesn't acknowledge me at first, her attention wholly fixed on the beach just outside her window.

A child with fawn brown hair splashes in the waves. She frolics and giggles in the water, finding an innocent, momentary respite in the grief that surrounds this home. She turns toward the window and my immortal gaze locks onto wide eyes of emerald green.

"She has your eyes." Selene's weak voice demands my attention. I drop to my knees at her bedside, taking her hands into mine.

"My light."

The sight of her like this, pale and barely clinging to life, enrages me. If I could kill Nobus, I would travel to the god realm right now and and rip his soul from his body with my bare hands.

But he made a deal with Creation that even my magic cannot undo.

"Have you come to take me home, Dark One?"

I nod my head, tears welling within me as her hand moves to my cheek. "I am sorry I could not come sooner. I am sorry that you had to suffer."

"I have many regrets, Drayven, but spending these years with her isn't one of them." The goddess cuts her eyes to the window as she speaks. "I've been waiting for her power to manifest, but it hasn't and I have no time left."

"It will," I whisper. "She is Light and Death. The daughter of two realms."

"Three," Selene corrects. "She is the daughter of three realms."

The goddess turns her attention toward the doorway and the sleeping human just down the hall.

There's a stabbing pain in my chest at the realization of how much Selene has grown to care for the mortal she married. I should be thankful for the life he gave her and our daughter, for the cover he provided for them both and the protection he offered them from Mikais. But I just want to kill him for having what I couldn't.

"Ansel will watch over Ivy. She will be safe with him."

"Ivy." I turn the name over in my mouth, the name of my daughter.

"Princess of the Under Realm and Goddess of the Umbra," Selene adds.

"Our little shadow has quite the name." I spare one last glance at the girl and the green dress that floats around her in the water. My magic calls out to the sea beast, summoning her to fulfill her bargain.

It is time, Arcasia. Mark her.

With the flick of her scaled tail, the sea beast swims towards the girl. Brown hair disappears under the current, destiny converging as the serpentine body of the Goddess of Protection grazes against her.

A child entered the sea, but it's a goddess who will emerge from its watery depths.

"It's time to go now, my light," I say, gently.

Selene sits up, slipping the silver ring from her thumb. She places it on the pillow—a token for the mortal husband she leaves behind.

I recognize the gesture and follow suit, slipping the flower from my pocket and setting it beside the ring. A sigil for the daughter who will have to navigate the ancient power in her veins without anyone to guide her.

"Godsbane," Selene whispers. "You remembered."

"Seems fitting for the dark bloom who bring gods to their knees, don't you think?"

She nods sadly, tears filling her golden eyes. Eyes that still sparkle despite Nobus' best efforts to dull them.

"Kill me, my love, so that I may finally be beside you for eternity." Selene places her hand in mine as what remains of her power ripples out in a blinding flash.

An eclipse washes away the light, the sun vanishing from the noonday sky. The shadow of a crescent moon splays across the sand as I wrap the Goddess of Light in my arms. My lips caress her skin, grazing gently across the constellation of freckles that decorate her cheekbones.

She may have been forgotten by the mortals, but I never forgot her. Not for a single second of the past eight agonizing years. And I will take my time reacquainting myself with every part of her.

I spare one last look at the child goddess crawling across the beach—soaking, trembling, and terrified.

The Prince of the Gods is not the only one who will be forged, broken, and remade by this realm. Today is the first of many trials she will face, but she will not be defeated.

Nobus fears what his son will become, but his fear is misplaced. She is a creature of the Under Realm, afterall. And one day, when she comes into her full power, baptized in fury and drenched in decades of rage, they will be the ones trembling.

"Drayven," Selene whispers weakly against my cheek. "Take me home now. "

The light from her golden eyes collides with mine in a kaleidoscope of shimmering magic. I call to my shadows, letting them wrap around us as my grip on her tightens.

"Your throne awaits, my queen."

EPILOGUE

SELENE

"Drayven."

I sigh as I enter his study. His desk is a mess, the top littered with scraps of used parchment and half-empty mugs of coffee, and whiskey, and Creation knows what else.

"What has gotten into you?"

"She should have been here by now." He lifts one of the mugs, taking a deep drink before spitting the cold liquid back into the vessel. His nose scrunches in disgust.

"You're sure it's today?"

"Yes, my light. I am sure it's today." Drayven tries and fails to hide his irritation at my question. "I am the Dark God of Death. I know when a name is added to the scroll of souls, especially when that name belongs to an immortal god of the Golden Pantheon."

"He always gets like this, Your Majesty." Corvus perches on the back of black leather chair where the god sits.

"Tell me again how you know she'll be here," I push.

Drayven's fingers tangle in his white hair as he sighs. He wants to resist my attempt to calm him by forcing him to recount the details he's already told me, but he rarely denies me anything I ask.

The dark purple blooms in the vase beside him wither as he expends a sliver of his infinite magic.

"Today's scroll contains so many names in one central location that it's nearly an offering to War. All soldiers, all in the palace where the Wolf God has taken residence. The Reapers have been tailing their little party and reporting back on how Ivy's power is growing. If Mikais' name is on the scroll today, that can only mean one thing."

There's an odd spark that flickers in his eyes when he talks about our daughter. Pride, tinged with a pinch of worry and a dash of regret. He would never admit to any of them, so instead of calling attention to it, I tuck it away in my heart.

"I told him it could be the boy, but he refuses to hear of it," Corvus chirps.

"It is *her*," Drayven growls. "She will overextend herself and the magic will bring her here. This is what it knows. This is its home." He pushes from the desk in an exasperated huff, the chair smacking the desk as he stands.

"If Mikais was dead, you would have felt it, right?" I ask, tentatively stepping toward him and placing my hands on the sides of his arms.

"Of course. The death of a god is felt in every realm."

"Okay, then we have time." I smile sweetly at him. "She will probably arrive in the throne room anyway. Why don't we walk that way together? It might calm your nerves."

"I do not have nerves."

Corvus lets out something that sounds like a chuckle at the god's continued denial. The noise, one I didn't know a raven could make, elicits several giggles from me before I can tamp my mouth shut.

"You two are insufferable together." Drayven groans. "Bird, you are not needed when the girl arrives."

"I think the girl might enjoy my comedic relief. Everyone loves an animal sidekick." The raven prances across the back of the chair, preening and shaking his iridescent feathers.

"The *girl* has a name," I chastise them both as I usher them out of the study and down the dimly lit halls of the palace.

"She does," Drayven agrees. "And she will also be terrified."

Terrified doesn't feel like a strong enough word for the emotions that will plague Ivy. If Death's deadly magic wasn't enough, there is also fire and grit and steel in her veins. She will be no better than a caged animal. Full of rage, coated in blood, and scared for her life. Not to mention the life of her fated that she will undoubtedly have left behind.

"Don't worry, Corvus. We will both get our chance to meet her one day." I stroke the raven on the head with my index finger, my memories filling with images of the young child I left behind. A girl who must be so different from the woman heading here today. "Why don't you go check on Amaya? She had a rough go in one of the mortal realms."

"Again? That Reaper cannot seem to stay out of trouble." The bird reluctantly flies off to investigate the fabricated incident, leaving me alone with my husband.

"It will be better this way, my light." Drayven offers me his elbow and I lace my arm through it as we stroll his halls. "The second she lands in this realm, she will be looking for a way out. There is information that she must know before she discovers she has the power to leave."

"I know." I smile sadly. "Finding out who she really is will be hard enough for her. A reunion would be too much."

Drayven leans in and plants a kiss on my temple. "She will be back, Selene. We aren't the only ones who will feel the Wolf God's death today."

A tear threatens to fall from my lashes. Today is the day that everything changes for our daughter. She found Calaedon and now his father will too. Nobus will feel Mikais' death and the location of the two gods we hid from him will finally be revealed.

"You're already dead, darling. There's nothing more he can do to you," Death reassures me.

"I am not worried about me. I am worried about them." I stop and turn to face him. "Maybe it's just a mother's intuition, but…I think she loves him the way I love you." Drayven pushes a golden curl from my face sweetly as the tear finally breaks free, streaking down my cheek. "But she will not run away like I did. She will stay and she will fight."

"You did fight, Selene." He takes my face between his hands, forcing my eyes to his. "They are only alive because of what you did."

"I didn't prepare her. I never told her what she was. I never told her to find him—"

"But he did," Drayven interrupts my spiraling thoughts. "He found her and he told her. I have watched her for years, countless trips to that Creation-foresaken realm." He shudders at the mention of the realm that held me prisoner.

"It doesn't matter how she got there, just that she did. In a realm that keeps gods nearly powerless, she has found enough magic to kill one." The smile that blooms on his face is filled with pride that he does not try to hide this time. "And one day, the Princess of the Under Realm will be the Queen of Shadows, ruler of the Golden Pantheon."

"Let's not get ahead of ourselves." I chuckle at the devious delight in his eyes. "Maybe just break the princess part to her today. The rest is merely your own speculation and ambition."

The ground beneath our feet trembles, the lights in the sconces flickering as a thunderous boom echoes through the realm.

"It's happening," Drayven says solemnly. "The Wolf God is dead."

"He could have used the doorbell." The joke falls flat, the god before me returning to a frenzied ball of tense energy. "Go on, get to the throne room, Your Majesty." Rising up on my toes, I place a kiss lightly on his cheek. "Go meet your daughter."

Drayven pats his pockets before his eyes snap to mine. "The flower. I wanted to bring her a flower." He returns the quick peck of a kiss and turns back toward the study.

"Drayven!" I call out for him but the Dark God doesn't stop. Instead he picks up the pace, his course set for the study and the godsbane he doesn't even realize he wilted.

Opening my palm, I grow the bloom's signature five midnight-hued sepals, the sigil of the daughter destined to save us all.

Unless, of course, she decides to destroy us instead.

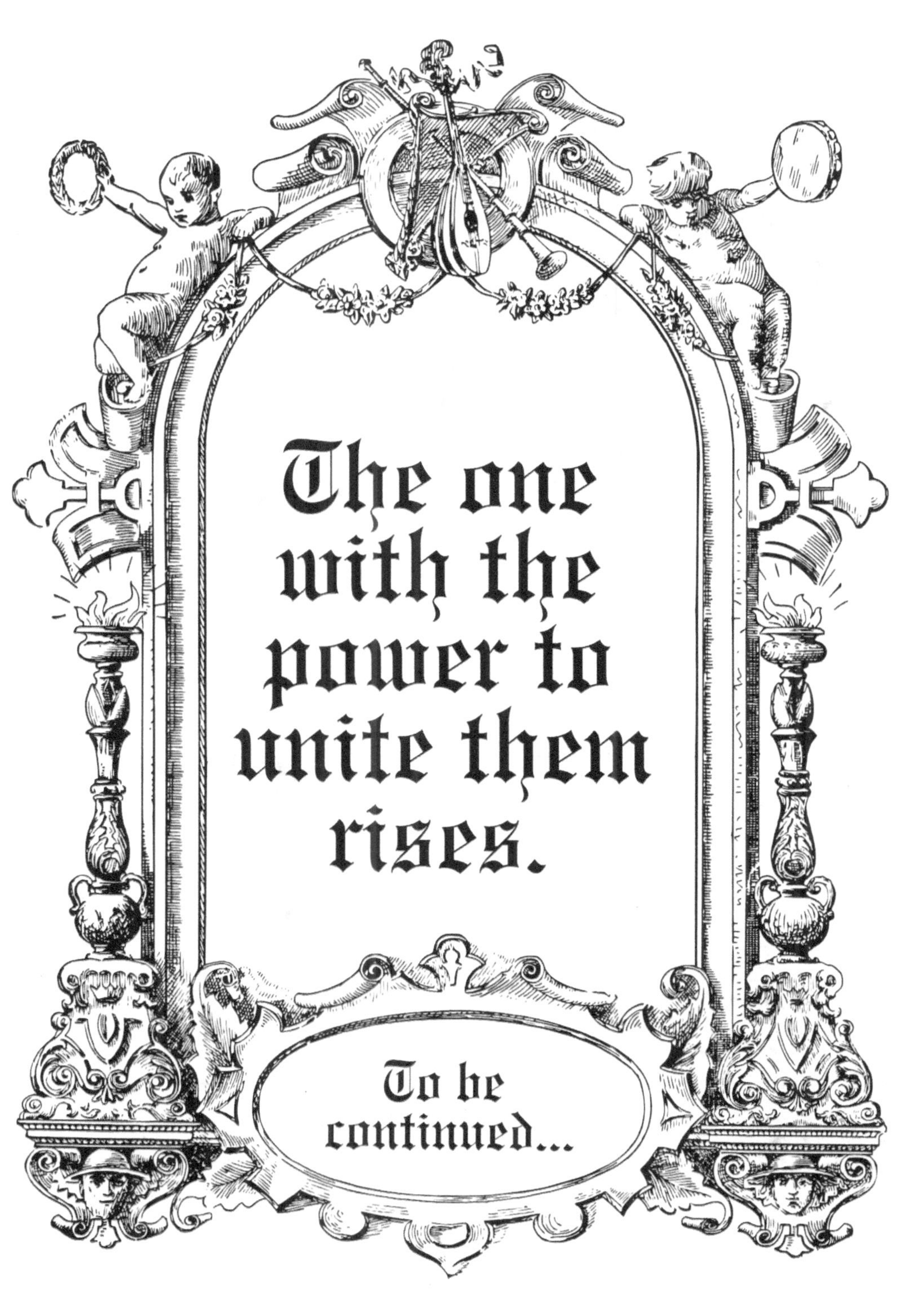

The one
with the
power to
unite them
rises.

To be
continued...

MUSINGS FROM THE AUTHOR

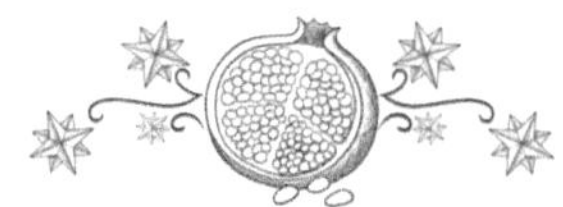

There are some stories that will not let you rest until you tell them. They wake you up in the middle of the night and weasel their way into every thing you do. I found myself doodling thoughts and ideas on grocery lists and in the margins of notebooks for a month before I finally caved and put Selene and Drayven's story on paper.

Godsbane was always Ivy's story, but it became clear to me while drafting book two that the beginning was just as important as the future. She was not the first to experience the cruel pull of fate, and she will not be the last.

This story, at its core, is a story of sacrifice, of love, and of loss. It's about two gods finally colliding after a millennia swirling in the other's orbit. It's about bargains made in secret to give the next generation a fighting chance. It's about the lengths a mother will go to for her children.

It's a drag path—evidence of love and forfeitures for the gods that come after them.

It's a way home.

There is still so much to explore in this world. Family, both found and blood, have a big role to play in what comes next. And I hope you'll stick around for the journey.

ACKNOWLEDGMENTS

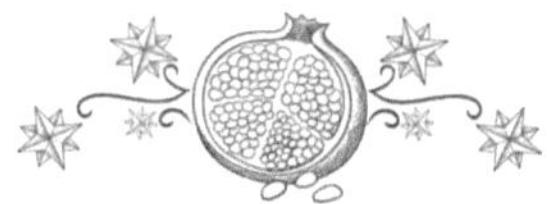

To Wil, who never balks when I say things like "I think I want to write a book over the holidays" and "I need to take a two day trip to the mountain so I can finish this."

To RK and WC, I would sacrifice every world for you both—and there's nothing I won't do to make this one better for you.

To Jerry's Angels, thank you for the support and for always listening to my ramblings and random lore dropping. You help me celebrate every win and you keep me going at my lowest. You're the best friends a gal can ask for.

To my dad, sorry for writing yet another book you cannot read. Mom will give you the summary.

To everyone who bought a copy of Godsbane, thank you for showing me that my dream can be something real. Your reviews, videos, and DMs have made me cry (in the best way) more times than I can count. I hope you love this story just as much.

To my ARC and street teams, you're the best hype crew around. I'm so lucky to have each and every one of you in my corner.

To the TikTok editors who share my love of Vecna and JCB, thank you for the inspiration for Drayven.

To MR, I know you'd be proud.

ABOUT THE AUTHOR

Lindsey Richardson is a self-proclaimed book dragon and lover of all things fantasy and romance. When she doesn't have her head buried in a book, you can find Lindsey at home crafting, spending time with her family and pets, cheering on the Tennessee Vols, and forcing her impeccable music taste on anyone who will listen.

Lindsey has dedicated her professional career to making a positive impact in the world through her favorite nonprofit organization. She is also an avid supporter of the Panhellenic experience.

Discover more of Lindsey's work and subscribe to her newsletter at www.lindseyrichardsonauthor.com